It looked like an innocent meeting at a coffee shop, but it couldn't be less innocent.

First, they waited for the authorities to do something.

They didn't.

Then they tried to wait it out, like good cops should.

They couldn't.

Now, it's time to get justice for their friends, cousins, brothers.

It was time to go North of the Border.

North of the Border:

Murder at
Punta Bandera Beach

By

A. E. Marta

Cover photos by Adalberto Marta
Text ©2011 by Adalberto E. Marta.
First Printing July 2, 2011

1. Cataloging in Publication data
2. Marta, A. E.
3. North of the Border: Murder at Punta Bandera Beach
4. p. cm.
5. ISBN 978-0-9755471-1-3

✝ **Divine Mercy Press** ✝
3216 Mission Avenue, Suite 138, Oceanside, California, 92058
5319 Willis Avenue, Dallas, Texas 75206
divinemercy@hypersurf.com
http//www.divinemercypress.com

North of the Border:

Murder at
Punta Bandera Beach

By

A. E. Marta

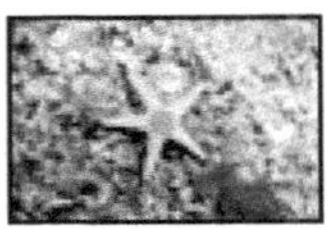

✝ Divine Mercy Press ✝
Dallas, Texas
Oceanside, California

This book is dedicated to my family and friends. Thank you for your unwavering support, understanding and faith.

"If I stand tall, it is because I am standing on the shoulders of those that came before me."
—African Proverb

Acknowledgement

To Doris Elaine Sauter, my editor and
publisher. Thank you for the inspiration,
persistence and faith.

Prologue:

Punta Bandera Beach,
Baja California
Spring, 2004

At two o'clock in the morning Punta Bandera Beach was deserted. Rhythmic sounds came from the small waves as they slowly hit the beach. The moon was visible far away in the sky. The shoreline was nearly covered in darkness; the white foam from the calm waves was barely visible on the surface of the sand.

A group of figures with dark clothes appeared from the dunes. With calculated steps they moved forward stopping at the edge of the water. From a backpack a person produced a high-power spotlight. Holding it by its contoured rubber grip he clicked the spotlight on and off three times. The high candle power beam was aimed out toward the ocean.

Another beam of light appeared through the darkness. It came from the ocean and it stayed on for a few seconds.

With precision, the group of people moved and spread out along the shoreline, keeping ten feet of distance between them, standing quietly. With everybody in place, the person holding the spotlight stood in the middle of the line, aiming the spotlight at the ocean, repeating the signal: the beam from the spotlight came on and off three times.

Two minutes later three small white-colored speed boats broke through the darkness and came into view; the high-power engines made a low humming sound. Three people were on each boat. Skillfully, the pilots maneuvered the boats close to the beach.

From the dunes, three dark-colored Suburban vehicles appeared, backing up and stopping about a hundred feet from the water. Stepping out of their vehicles, the drivers walked to the rear, opened the doors and stood at attention facing the water.

While the pilots kept the boats close to the water's edge, the assistants unloaded water-tight plastic containers. They were placed on the water and then pushed towards the shore. On cue, the line of people waiting on the beach walked into the ocean to meet the objects. With accuracy the items were carefully loaded into the Suburban vehicles.

No one exchanged words; it was all business.

After the containers were unloaded, one by one, the pilots moved the boats back a few yards before making a u-turn, creating a wide arch. It was all synchronized; the boats followed each other keeping a safe distance between them. The humming from the engines decreased as the boats disappeared back into the darkness.

Once the back doors of the Suburban automobiles were secured, the drivers got inside their cars, and, keeping a safe distance, the vehicles pulled away. The exchange of plastic containers between the two groups had taken less than nine minutes. Ten objects had been loaded into each Suburban car; each item contained five kilos of cocaine. One hundred and fifty kilos of cocaine had been unloaded from the boats and placed into the Suburban vehicles.

With the task completed, the group of workers walked back towards the dunes and disappeared.

Maintaining a safe distance from the beach, three people had observed the exchange of containers take place. They were Americans. The tallest had short gray hair, trimmed military style. He was holding a walkie-talkie. The bulk from a holster was noticeable through his windbreaker. Next to him, holding a cylindrical-shaped flashlight, stood a tall, thin person with well-groomed blond hair, wearing round wire-rim glasses. Behind them, wearing a San Diego baseball cap was a strongly built person, also armed and wearing a dark Adidas warm-up jacket.

It was a practice to stay behind after everybody else had departed. Patrols had been posted along the north and south parts of the beach and none of the groups had reported problems. Forming a triangle the Americans walked to the beach and stood still near the water. The only noise came from the waves coming in. They gazed along both sides of the shoreline but there was nothing to see; it was dark along the beach. With confident movements the trio walked back towards their vehicle hidden from view behind the dunes.

Before the trio reached the vehicle a loud command came through the handheld walkie-talkie.

"Wait!"

The command reverberated against the wind of the dark morning. The voice came from people patrolling the north side of the beach. Adrenaline rushed into their blood systems. The trio stopped and turned towards the north area.

A second command came out of the walkie-talkie.

"Stop!"

The call was ignored again.

The two Americans unzipped their jackets, and pulled out their 9mm Glock weapons. They kept them pressed to the back of their right legs, away from view. The blond man just stood still, holding the flashlight, waiting for somebody to make the next move. Quickly the gray-haired man raised his left hand and spread his fingers out.

Be quiet and don't move.

Taking the lead, he motioned his associates to keep walking. The trio walked about fifty feet and stopped, waiting for the person who called them to make an appearance.

From the shadows an armed group of Mexicans came forward gripping two men by their upper arms. When the group got close they fanned out, placing the two men in custody in front of the Americans. A Mexican carrying a pair of night vision goggles turned on a small hand-held flashlight, illuminating the two hostages. The captives were barefooted and shirtless. Large bruises were visible along their rib cages. Both had bleeding cuts on their foreheads and cheeks. One had a slanted jaw; it was broken in two places. The duct tape placed across their mouths gave them a grotesque appearance. Their hands had been tied behind their backs with white plastic ties. Sweat was running down the front and sides of their faces. Their dark eyes kept darting back and forth as they blinked. Blood, mixed with sweat, was visible near their hairlines.

The man with the San Diego baseball cap stood near the Mexicans, observing the group. He was hiding his weapon behind his right leg, ready to use it.

Placing his Glock behind his waist, the tall gray-haired man looked at the group and then at the captives. With a stern gaze he asked the Mexican holding the hand-held flashlight, "Where did you find them?"

Pointing north with the flashlight the Mexican answered, "We found them less than half a mile from here . . . from what we have gathered they came here to camp for the weekend." He paused and then looked at the hostages. "I think we have a problem with these guys . . . I am almost sure they are local police officers . . . they have Rosarito Police badges. If we—"

Moving his head in disapproval, the tall American cut off the person in mid-sentence, "I don't care who they are. Get rid of them."

Swiftly, the American put the Glock back in its holster and carefully zipped his windbreaker back up. Glancing at his partner with the baseball cap he said, "Put your gun away." Turning towards the vehicle parked in the dunes he said to his associates, "Let's go."

The Mexican holding the flashlight didn't move; he was shocked by the reaction of the American. Looking at the hostages and at the rest of the people in his group he said to no one in particular, "I don't know if we should do anything to these guys. If they are local police officers things can get complicated."

"It doesn't matter," replied the tall gray-haired man with a tone of annoyance in his voice, still walking towards the vehicle.

The guy with the baseball cap and the blond man just stood there, looking at the desperate, sweaty faces of the two hostages, and then at their associate's back, unable to move. They were stunned by their friend's carefree attitude towards the two hostages. In all their years together nobody had been killed in cold blood.

Placing his weapon away the man with the baseball cap turned to his companion and said, "I don't like it, but the decision has been made. Let's go."

The blond man didn't move. Looking at the hostages again and then towards his two friends walking away, he implored, "Do we have to kill them?" Without waiting for a reply he added, "Hey! Let's not do anything stupid! If they are police officers from Rosarito we can't just have them killed! Shit, Tom, we'll be in a real mess!" He remained standing, limbs akimbo, waiting for an answer.

The group of Mexicans looked at each other. Should they stay or go?

The man with the baseball cap continued walking towards the car, embarrassed by his friend's lack of conviction. He considered going back to grab the guy by the collar and drag him back to the car, but decided against it.

The gray-haired man had reached the vehicle when he heard his business partner call his name.

His initial reaction was to ignore him, get inside the car and start the engine. If his partner insisted on being a Good Samaritan, he'd leave without him; the spineless fuck could walk back across the border for all he cared.

For years loads of money had been made trading drugs along the border and each time without delay, or complaints from the group. Why the hell is this son of a bitch questioning his judgment now?

With firm steps, he returned to where the blond man and the group of Mexicans were standing. With a mean look on his face and in a harsh voice he addressed the group.

"This is a fucking high-risk business and those two guys can screw things up for all of us." Pointing his finger he continued, "If we let them go, they will go back to Rosarito and inform the local police what we did here this morning. Then a shit-load of federal officers will be looking for us. We can't afford to have any loose ends." Tapping his fingers on his friend's chest, he added, "Did you understand what I've said, or do you want me to explain it in another way?"

Without waiting for a reply he pointed to the group of Mexicans holding the two hostages and without emotion repeated his command, "Get rid of them."

Taking long steps he turned towards his vehicle.

The blond man hesitated. First he looked at his friend walking away and then to the group of Mexicans. Taking a couple of steps he approached the Mexican holding the flashlight and said something to him. He moved his arms and hands to accentuate his point and pointed to the north.

The Mexican listened attentively and then nodded his head in affirmation. Lifting the flashlight he turned towards the group, and pointing north said, "Let's take them back to their tents."

One

Playas de Rosarito, Baja California
Saturday December 19, 2009

At five-thirty in the morning faint rays of sunlight were shooting up at the dark sky from behind the eastern hills of Rosarito. Along Avenida Benito Juarez, the four-lane avenue of the downtown area, silhouettes of pedestrians were visible moving on the narrow concrete sidewalks. Neon signs advertising restaurants, hotels, bars and pharmacies were visible on both side of the avenue. People stood in front of taco stands; some eating their meals, others waiting to place their orders.

La Tortuga Restaurant, located along Rosarito's main boulevard, was ready for business. Two waiters arranged four chairs to a table; another unfolded a white linen tablecloth, quickly placed it on the table and smoothed the creases with the open palms of his hands; a fourth waiter placed clear plastic vases with fresh flowers on the center of each table. The smell and sounds of meat and vegetables sizzling on pans, fresh coffee brewing, and banter coming from the large kitchen, permeated the restaurant.

Sitting at a table by the large window, which encompassed the entire east side of the restaurant, Rosarito Municipal Police officers Javier Ortega and David Avalos, dressed in civilian clothes, were drinking Colombian coffee, talking about the coming local elections, waiting for their guest to arrive.

Don Ramon, the owner of the restaurant, allowed the two police officers to come in and have coffee, breakfast, and hold meetings, before the restaurant was open for business.

The restaurant was located on the second floor, above a pharmacy, an ice cream store, and a bakery. From their table the two police officers had a commanding view of Avenida Juarez. At the moment the front parking lot was empty but in a few hours hundreds of tourists from north of the border were going to fill the main avenue of the town. Playas de Rosarito is tucked between Tijuana and Ensenada, along the Baja California coast.

Coming from the north, a small light blue car traveling on the right lane of the main avenue started to slow down. The car's right turn signal light started to blink. The vehicle turned into the parking lot, found a parking stall and slowly came to a stop. A man wearing a dark blue jacket, jeans and running shoes, got out of the car. Pointing to the car he activated the alarm with the clicker, and then headed for the front stairway leading to the restaurant. A folded newspaper was in his right hand. With slow steps he walked up the stairs and when he reached the top he pulled the tall wooden doors open and walked in.

Nervous, Javier and David observed the man walk up the steps and open the doors of the restaurant. Both got up from their chairs to greet the visitor. Javier was the first one to embrace him. The guest was Detective Manny Ortiz, Javier's cousin. Manny was an officer with the San Diego Police Department. Together the trio walked back to the table.

Manny gazed out the window. The morning light had almost risen over the mountains, showering the sky with colors of blue, yellow and orange. With an uneasy smile Manny said, "Man, what a sight. Everything looks beautiful from here."

Less tense, David answered, "We know. That's why we love coming here in the morning,"

Manny stared out the window a few more seconds, then turned to Javier and David and waited for them to start the conversation.

"Manny, thank you for coming," Javier said, as he signaled one of the waiters and motioned for an extra cup of coffee.

"No problem. Happy to be here," Manny replied nodding his head. He waited for the young waiter to finish pouring the coffee into his cup before continuing. When the waiter left, he pulled a manila envelope from inside the folded newspaper and placed it on the table.

"Guys—you did well," Manny said matter-of-factly.

With the same expression on his face he added, "We know who they are and where they live. I got names, addresses, and photos of the guys who killed Luis and Ramiro at Punta Bandera Beach."

Carefully Manny poured cream and sugar into his coffee cup and with a spoon stirred the contents to his taste. Slowly he took a sip of the coffee and then placed the cup on the table. He waited for Javier to take the envelope.

"Go ahead, take the papers out of the envelope," he urged.

Javier reached for the manila envelope. It was thin but felt heavy. He removed the contents from the envelope. The first photograph showed a serious-looking person with short gray hair looking directly at the camera. The California and American flags were displayed in the background. His name was Thomas Peterson, and he was an active Drug Enforcement Agency agent living in Encinitas and working out of a downtown San Diego office. His birth date was inscribed with blue ink at the bottom of the picture.

The next photograph had the same background and it showed an individual in a green uniform, smiling, looking past the camera. His brown hair was beginning to recede along his forehead. His name was Samuel Anderson, an active Border Patrol officer living in Fallbrook and working at the Temecula Border Patrol checkpoint. His birth date was also inscribed at the bottom of the picture.

The last photo was of a blond, well-groomed individual wearing an expensive dark blue suit with a blue tie and gold-rimmed glasses. His name was Stewart Connors, a banker. He lived in Rancho Santa Fe and worked out of an office in Del Mar. Javier scanned the background information without emotion. Using both hands he made one single stack and passed the material to David. As Javier and Manny drank their coffee and talked about their families, David processed the information.

When David finished reading he placed everything back inside the manila envelope. Manny raised his hand to signal the waiter for more coffee and then leaned forward and said, "The license plate numbers and other information you guys gave me were correct. We have two federal officers and a banker making drug deals on both sides of the border. Can you believe that shit?

Javier and David smiled but did not answer; it was a rhetorical question. The conversation stopped when the young waiter came to refill their coffee cups. For the next few seconds the table became quiet; they concentrated on their coffee. Javier placed his coffee cup back on the table and grabbed the manila envelope with both hands. Looking at Manny, he said, "I have no right to ask for more favors, but I am going to ask anyway."

Manny took a sip of his coffee; his head slightly moving up and down as if he had already anticipated the question. Holding the cup of coffee he said, "What else can I help you with?"

Javier became concerned. His request placed Manny in a dangerous position; it made him an accomplice to a crime. "Before you answer, please think about the consequences. Being a San Diego Police officer, it can compromise you. I don't want to hurt you, your family, or your career."

Manny's face became serious; he seemed to concentrate on the predicament. After a few seconds he said, "OK, go ahead and ask."

With apprehension Javier asked, "We need a vehicle and two guns. Remember, we can't return the car or the weapons."

Without hesitation Manny replied, "I had a feeling you would." With his right hand he reached inside his jacket and produced a small white envelope.

"There are two keys inside; one is for the ignition and the other for the trunk. The car is a wine-color Volvo 240 DL and it's parked at my mom's house. She knows what's going on. The registration and insurance card are secured on the inside part of the visor on the driver's side. Check the trunk of the car carefully; I am sure you will find what you need in there. I bought the car for my mother at a public sale about two years ago but she doesn't like to drive anymore. The car is registered in her name, so don't worry about being stopped by the police. She wants you guys to use the car."

Using both hands Javier opened one end of the envelope and tipped it. The keys dropped on the table. Holding the keys he said, "Manny, we can never repay you for all you have done. When this is over I want all of us to get together and have a family reunion again. But right now, I am worried. After you finish your coffee I want you to go home. You never know who's watching . . . we'll take it from here."

"I'm done with my coffee," Manny said, standing up, allowing Javier and David to do the same. "It was great talking to both of you again." He hugged Javier and did the same with David. "Please remember, if you need anything, I am here for you."

"Thank you, cousin," Javier said, with a soft smile on his lips.

David smiled, nodding in affirmation.

The three of them walked to the door of the restaurant. Holding the door open, Manny turned to wave goodbye and then walked down the steps.

Javier and David returned to their table. David signaled the waiter and said, "More coffee, please."

The young waiter filled their cups with fresh coffee and walked away. Taking their time both placed cream and sugar in their coffees.

David was the first to talk. "Are you surprised about the two federal officers and the banker?"

"At first I was confused, but once you think about it, it makes sense. It's easy for the federal officers to move across the border and the banker takes care of the money. It's a good system," Javier answered.

"I know money will corrupt almost anybody, including the Pope, but I'm still surprised and disappointed two federal officers are involved," David said, taking a sip of his coffee.

Javier didn't respond; he remained lost in thought.

Looking at his friend David asked, "I know you want to be alone to read the information again. Are we doing anything in particular the rest of the day?"

"No. I'm going to stay here a few more minutes and then go home to rest. Let's meet here tomorrow morning and talk about a plan." Javier answered, rubbing the rim of the cup of coffee with his right thumb.

Gazing out the window, David said, "Going to San Diego for a few days is going to be painful for our families."

"I know," replied Javier with a somber look on his face. For five years Javier and David had placed their families in insecure situations more than once. This time it was different. Crossing the border to arrest United States citizens increased the repercussions for everybody many times over.

David understood Javier's somber mood. From any angle, two local police officers matching wits against two United States Federal Agents was not a good contest; it was a suicide mission. Taking the last sip of his coffee, David said, "I'm going home; I need to talk to my mother and sister." Without waiting for an answer David got up, moved the chair against the table and headed for the door.

Out in the parking lot, David got into his car and carefully maneuvered the vehicle around the building and onto Avenida Juarez. As the car moved along the avenue he was planning how to explain the police information to his mother and sister. With care he removed his cell phone from its case and dialed his mother's home phone number. After exchanging pleasantries he announced he was coming over and bringing breakfast. Four blocks later he pulled over and parked in front of *La Huerta* Restaurant, his mother's favorite eating place. He ordered generous servings of scrambled eggs, beans, bacon and tortillas. While waiting for the food he called his girlfriend. He said he was having breakfast with his family and asked her to meet him at his house later in the morning. Bags of food in hand, he returned to his car and drove south along the avenue again. At Calle Venustiano Carranza, he made a right turn. Three blocks later he parked the car in front of his mother's house.

When David arrived, Irma Avalos, a woman in her late sixties, was sitting on the sofa in the living room, pretending to watch the local morning news. She became apprehensive after her son's phone call. The last time her son visited and brought breakfast with him was when David was accepted to the Federal Police Academy in Mexicali. To her all the federal police officers were morally corrupted and full of greed and now her son was part of the same group she despised.

With a smile on her face Mrs. Avalos got up from the sofa. David stood by the door and waited for his mother's hug and a kiss. Together they walked to the kitchen. While his mother unpacked the food from the paper bags, David set up the table. Susana, David's younger sister, emerged from her bedroom. She was holding the house phone in her right ear. Smiling, she walked over to the dinning room area, hugged David and then gave him a kiss. She walked over to the kitchen and using her right shoulder to hold the phone close to her ear, grabbed a tortilla, placed it on the open palm of her left hand, and rolled the tortilla into a thin roll in one single motion. She took a bite of the tortilla, smiled at

David in a sign of approval, and without breaking stride, walked back to the bedroom.

Minutes later they sat at the table enjoying their food, talking about the coming elections and the possibility of the former police chief becoming the town's next mayor. Susana talked about the increased bureaucracy at her office in the Small Business Bureau in Tijuana, and the coming Christmas and New Year's celebrations. When they finished their breakfast David said he had information to share. For their protection he asked them to listen, and to refrain from asking questions.

In simple language he explained the police work Javier and he had performed the last five years. How they had spied on people in bars and restaurants in Rosarito and Tijuana, by the Mesa de Otay area. Using reliable information from police reports and witnesses, they had arrested and interrogated suspects in the outskirts of Rosarito. They had hurt people. This morning, Javier's cousin gave them information about two federal agents and a banker living in San Diego, the people responsible for the deaths of Luis Hernandez and Ramiro Flores. The plan was to drive north of the border and arrest the federal agents and the banker next week. Looking his mother in the eyes, he asked her to pray and to have faith. Turning to his sister, he asked her to move in with her mother for one week.

When David stopped talking the table became silent. Seconds later his mother covered her face with her hands and began to cry, her head slightly tilting forward. Susana moved her chair next to her mother and hugged her in a tender embrace. David wanted to hold his mother and sister but he knew he shouldn't; his action would prolong the agony all of them felt. With a heavy heart David got up from his chair, pulled the chair away from the table, and slowly pushed the chair back. Quietly, he walked out of the house, got into his car and drove back to Avenida Juarez.

Two

Javier waved to a waiter and ordered more coffee. Even though he was mentally exhausted he decided to stay and write down the thoughts floating in his head. With renewed enthusiasm he opened the manila envelope and spread the contents on the table. Taking a pen from his shirt pocket he began to scribble notes on the back of the manila envelope.

As the note-taking progressed a breakfast plate was placed on the table. The smell of eggs and bacon was difficult to ignore. He moved the papers and the manila envelope to the edge of the table and placed the breakfast plate in front of him. Before eating, he looked towards the kitchen, and when he made eye contact with Don Ramon, he nodded his head as a "thank you" gesture. Don Ramon smiled back and then continued talking with one of the cooks, while carefully slicing large red tomatoes into thin slices.

While eating Javier contemplated possible scenarios once they crossed the border into San Diego County. On the surface, crossing the border into San Diego to arrest federal officers was madness; especially if they tried to arrest the federal agents out in the street and in plain daylight. Javier felt confident because they had two factors in their favor: nobody knew who they were, and no one expected them.

They had to cross the border into San Ysidro on Monday morning and return by Thursday or Friday at the latest. Once in San Diego he was sure they could keep Thomas Peterson under surveillance without being detected. Thomas would lead them to the other two guys.

Javier dropped the fork and grabbed the pen to cross out and rewrite words he had written on the corner of the manila envelope. He stopped writing, and remained still for a few seconds. Slowly, fear began to creep into his chest. His breathing became shallow and uneven. Tightness began to squeeze his chest and the fingers of both hands felt numb and began to tingle. It was a panic attack; he had experienced one before. He was not afraid of dying, but leaving his wife without a husband and his daughter without a father was something he couldn't face. To control his anxiety he fixed his eyes on the world outside the restaurant. Along the main avenue cars with local and California license plates drove by. Transit buses, emitting large clouds of black diesel smoke from their silver-painted mufflers, moved in opposite directions, and pedestrians, moving at a fast pace, appeared eager to reach their destinations. He closed his eyes for a few seconds. A minute later, he felt better.

After returning the contents back to the manila envelope, he reached for his wallet, pulled out forty dollars and placed them on the table. With ease he carried the plate to the kitchen and gave it to one of the busboys. On his way out he waved goodbye to the restaurant workers and Don Ramon.

Outside in the parking lot he decided to go for a walk along the beach next to the Rosarito Beach Hotel before going home to his family. Driving south along the avenue he noticed the morning traffic was not heavy. At the entrance of the Rosarito Beach Hotel he turned in and parked in front of a clothing store. He locked the car and walked past the shops and restaurants, heading towards the beach area.

Javier wanted to feel and taste the salty breeze on his face and hear the sound of the waves coming to the shore. He walked along the beach lost in thought, looking at the endless shoreline rising and falling in the distance, feeling his shoes sink into the soft, wet sand with each step. At one point he stopped and faced the ocean, concentrating on the infinite imaginary line, the point where the ocean meets the sky, and wondered if he was ever going to return to this place again. After a twenty minute walk he returned to his car thoughtful, but not afraid.

On the way home Javier rolled down the window of the car. For five miles he saw cars and taxis zigzagging along the main avenue; fellow police officers directing traffic; and animated families and tourists walking along the streets.

When he pulled to the front of his house, the family dog came running out to greet him. The dog sat on his hind legs, eagerly waiting for his customary rub on the head. As Javier kneeled down to scratch the dog's head, he could hear his wife somewhere in the backyard laughing, having an energetic conversation with one of their neighbors.

After entering the house he walked to the kitchen, opened the refrigerator door and grabbed a bottle of water. Holding the bottle he moved to the bedroom and sat on the edge of the bed. Between sips of water his eyes concentrated on the twenty-four by thirty-six inch photo frame hanging from the wall. The frame was full of photographs, placed randomly in the form of a collage. The photographs were of his daughter, wife and himself, at different stages of their lives. Close to the center of the frame was a photograph of Javier and his cousin, Luis Hernandez, both as teenagers. The date the photograph was taken was engraved in Javier's mind; he had just turned thirteen and Luis was twenty-one years old.

The year was 1970; a lifetime ago.

The sound of the front screen door opening and closing and the soft steps of his wife approaching released Javier from his spell. Angelica stopped at the door and leaned against the frame, arms crossed, holding her elbows with her hands.

Minutes ago she was having an animated conversation with her neighbor, but now her face was pale, full of worry. After her husband had left the house early this morning, she had cried for a while. She was confused; a nervous wreck. She wanted to slap her husband, yell at him for placing the family in danger. If her husband got killed, how was she supposed to move on with her life? How would she support her daughter and herself without a job?

But she also felt guilty. The wives of Luis and Ramiro, killed at Punta Bandera Beach five years ago, had been forced to go on with their lives after their husbands were killed.

They didn't have a choice.

Who was she, to demand better treatment from life?

She had kept busy cleaning the house and helping the wife of a neighbor's select curtain material for her living room window. Anticipating a somber conversation with her husband, she had sent their daughter to spend the weekend with her own parents in Ensenada late yesterday.

Angelica had mentally rehearsed for this moment for a long time and now she found it difficult to control her emotions. She didn't know what to say or how to start. There were questions to ask about the investigation and this morning's meeting. But she understood her situation; the less the family knew, the lower the danger. She stayed leaning against the door frame, looking at her husband, waiting.

Javier was the first to break the silence. "All I can tell you is this: we have the names and addresses of the people responsible for the deaths of Luis and Ramiro. They are Americans; a Border Patrol agent, a federal drug enforcement agent, and a banker."

Angelica's heart skipped a beat and her eyes became fully dilated. She had to use all her strength to keep her composure.

Javier continued, "I don't know what I am going to do when I find them. Five years ago I dreamed of torturing every one of them. I would break every bone in their bodies, starting with their toes. Shoot them in the liver and then dump their bodies someplace far away to let them die a painful, slow death. But that was five years ago. I am not sure anymore."

"If you are not going to kill them, are you going to turn them in?" Angelica's voice came out slow and soft.

"Early this morning I had in mind to turn them in, but I am not sure what David and I are going to do. I wish I could give you plans with information and lots of details, but I can't. I am sorry." Javier answered, looking at the wall, instead of his wife.

With apprehension she asked, "Are we in danger? Should we move in with my parents?"

Javier stood up and answered, "Yes. David and I are crossing the border into San Ysidro Monday morning and we are stopping at one place. At the first chance we get we'll grab the two federal officers first and then the banker. We are going to be followed back to Rosarito. Friends of the federal officers will come here to retaliate."

Angelica didn't answer, but her brain was

making rapid calculations: two police officers from the small town of Rosarito lacking resources, sophisticated investigative skills, weapons and self-defense training, against two U.S. federal officers and a banker? It was madness!

Javier sensed Angelica's desperation, "I know what you are thinking, but I want you to believe in me. I am placing you, our daughter, and the rest of our families in danger, but it has to be done. After years of searching for the killers of Luis and Ramiro we can't stop and just let it go. I can't move on with my life until we get closure, one way or another."

Angelica wanted to scream, to unleash all the pain inside her chest, but she knew it was pointless; the wheels of Javier's view of justice had been set in motion five years ago and it was too late to stop it now. Moving away from the door frame, she walked to her husband, knelt down, gently placed her arms around him and hugged him tight, but did not cry. She was going to be strong for him and their daughter. She believed in her husband because throughout their years together Javier had delivered on every promise he made. Deep inside her soul there was a gleam of hope Javier would come back to them alive, and she was going to hang on to that hope for as long as possible.

Three

Vista, California
Saturday December 19, 2009

Frank was in a deep sleep, having one of those dreams that feels good and sounds good, but doesn't make sense. He was inside a shiny blue sports car driving at a surrealistically high speed, which was odd because he never drove past the legal limit. The sports car was low to the ground and the dashboard had many knobs and switches. Wind was blowing his hair all over the place.

The car must be European.

He was driving through a town located up on a hill. The houses were old, made out of large adobe bricks with Mexican tile roofs, blending properly with the earth. The streets were narrow; people and houses becoming a blur as the car zoomed past them. The open road became wide and then narrowed with sharp turns that straightened out as the car moved along. Portions of greenery appeared by the side of the road, maybe trees and tall plants, it was difficult to tell because the wind made it hard to turn and look to the side. Darkness covered the road and the sky for a few seconds.

Was that a tunnel, or a large cloud?

Frank was still driving the sports car when a phone's faint ringing began to separate him from the dream. The phone kept ringing, the noise increasing with each ring. He opened his eyes for a split second and right away he wished he hadn't. The sides of his head began to pound and the ceiling of the room started to rotate.

The phone continued to ring.

With incredible effort he reached the edge of the bed, picked up the phone from the floor and held it to the side of his head.

"Hello?" Frank's voice came out rough and dry.

"Frank, it's ten in the morning!" The words at the other end of the phone came out loud and clear. "You promised me you would be here at seven!" The voice was full of irritation.

"Who's this?" Frank's words came out slurred; his brain was unable to process the information.

"You are three hours late!"

Frank recognized the caller. "Shit!" Frank yelled at the phone, then did his best to sit up. The room was moving; everything was out of focus.

"Are you coming to work?" The caller was less irritated.

"I overslept but I'm on my way right now. Give me five minutes to get ready and I'm on my way. I'm terribly sorry. I'll be there in a few minutes."

"Listen, Frank. You need to be here in thirty minutes, or you don't have a job. Do you understand?"

Frank tried to reply but the phone line was already dead.

Frank sat in bed leaning forward holding his head in his hands; his mouth started to collect bile and the pounding in his head was getting louder.

Dragging his feet, he walked to the bathroom and bent over the sink to spit out the bile that had pooled inside his mouth. With shaky hands Frank turned on the cold water faucet. Using both hands he collected water from the faucet and slurped some of it to rinse out the sour taste from his mouth. He collected more cold water, threw it against his face, and with wet fingers combed his dirty hair. When he lifted his head to look into the mirror, a face with bloodshot eyes and a head with tangled, wet and oily hair came into view.

With tentative steps he walked out of the bathroom and into the bedroom. He grabbed his T-shirt from the floor and brought it close to his face. It smelled of sweat and cigarette smoke. He was sure he didn't have a clean T-shirt somewhere inside the dresser. Putting on the soiled T-shirt, he headed towards the kitchen to find the truck keys and his cigarettes. Standing by the kitchen sink he did his best to remember, but there was no recollection of the empty beer bottles on the floor, the cigarette ashes on the couch or the leftover food still on the counter next to the sink. A small plastic container of salsa had opened and spilled on the floor.

There was a new pack of cigarettes sticking out from under his work jacket lying on the floor, and the truck keys were next to it. In one single motion he bent and grabbed the pack of cigarettes and the set of keys and walked out the door.

On his way to Fallbrook, Frank opened the pack of cigarettes, took one out and lit it with his Zippo lighter. Sweat was beginning to form on his forehead; maybe he wasn't going to get sick after all.

John Harrison and his company, Terranova Construction of San Diego, had been designing and building custom homes for selected customers in the

San Diego and Riverside Counties since 1967. Last year, Paul Murphy, the company's handyman, retired after twenty-five years of service. Replacing Paul had been a top priority for the company but they had not been able to find a first-class candidate. Ten months ago Frank showed up at one of their job sites looking for free leftover wood. John told him he could have all the wood he wanted provided he hauled away two truckloads of trash. John was willing to pay two hundred dollars for the use of Frank's truck, plus fifty dollars for gasoline, and another fifty dollars to pay the landfill's fee. For Frank the deal was just too good to pass up.

After that day a gentleman's agreement was made: John offered two hundred and fifty dollars per day, fifty dollars for the use of the truck, plus expenses. Frank was required to keep track of all the receipts and to turn them in with an invoice after completing each job.

The arragnment was the beginning of a love and hate relationship between John and Frank. Even though Frank had not been hired as an official company worker or as a subcontractor, John had always done his best to provide him with steady work. Frank in return, had done his best to arrive late to work on a regular basis. John was in a quandary: on the one hand he respected Frank's ability to endure long work hours and his attitude towards detail when completing each job. On the other hand, getting Frank to each project on time was a challenge.

Frank made it to Fallbrook in less than thirty minutes and after parking his truck next to a pile of trash he went to work right away. After a few minutes of physical labor his stomach began to feel better and the pounding in his head was diminishing. He was beginning to work up a sweat when John showed up.

"Good morning. I'm glad you made it, Frank." At seventy years of age John Harrison was still an imposing figure. He was a person with a strong faith in people anchored on basic principles: your word is your bond, and you never promise something you can't deliver.

Frank moved closer. "John . . . I'm sorry about being late this morning. I know that you—"

John raised his hand, index finger pointed up.

"Frank, just listen—don't talk."

Frank removed his work gloves and stood at attention; he wanted to say something but decided not to.

"If you have any comments please wait until I'm done."

"OK." Frank said, taking a couple of steps back.

"We are officially closing down for business today. With Christmas and the New Year just around the corner we need time off for the holidays and for inventory. I'll be around for the next three or four days. I'm meeting with potential home buyers, with subcontractors and with some of our bankers; a couple of banks are worried about our solvency but we are fine, there is nothing to worry about. After the business meetings I'm flying north to Sacramento to be with my family." There was a pause. John was looking for the correct words to frame the next part of his speech.

"I'm making changes next year. And some of those changes relate to you."

There was another pause. "You need to change your behavior, your attitude towards work and this company. I honestly don't care what you do in your private life but starting next year, I want you to be on time—all the time. I also want you to look respectable when you show up for work, not like a fucking bum. I'm sorry about my language, Frank, but I just don't know how to reach you, how to make you understand the seriousness of the situation."

"Come on, John." Frank responded, hoping to look insulted. "Look, I got my work boots, jeans and a T-shirt. I mean, what do you want, a suit and a tie?"

"Frank, the problem you have is this: there is always a reason, a motive for everything you do, or everything that happens to you. You don't take responsibility for your actions. Look at you. Right now you look like shit. You still smell of alcohol, sweat, and cigarettes."

John reached into the left front pocket of his shirt and removed two folded pieces of paper. Looking at the papers, and then at Frank, he said, "Frank, it's your life, your decision. Now let's talk about money. I reviewed the receipts and invoices and other papers you gave me three days ago and according to my calculations, I owe you eighteen hundred dollars. That does not include the Johnson's job, and of course, this one." John made a pause in order to reorganize the papers he had in his hand.

"Give me the invoices for the Johnson's and this one, and I'll reimburse you. But you have to do it soon. Like I said, I'm leaving in the next few days for Sacramento."

John pulled out an envelope from his pants back pocket and handed it to Frank.

"There is a check for eighteen hundred dollars plus a bonus. I am giving you a couple of thousand dollars in the spirit of Christmas. No, that's not true . . ." John placed his hands on his hips and then looked at Frank straight in the eyes

"I'm giving you the extra money because you deserve it. You are one hell of a worker, Frank, and you have earned the money. You can go far in this company. I don't want to lose you."

John's bluntness made Frank feel guilty. "Thanks, John."

"Well, I have to go. If I don't see you next week, have a good Christmas, all right?"

"You, too, John. Please say hello to the family."

"Frank, don't forget the invoices for the Johnson's job. It's about five hundred dollars worth of receipts plus whatever you're going to spend for this one."

"I'll get the receipts and turn in the invoices, John."

Frank let out a sigh; everything John had said was true and Frank knew it. God, he was embarrassed because John had taken good care of him for many months and he had let him down.

I'm not going to disappoint him again, Frank said to himself, as he placed the envelope with the money inside his right front pant pocket.

With the dedication reserved for new employees determined to impress their boss, Frank removed the rubble from the house in Fallbrook in under seven hours. No time was taken for the customary burger, soda and fries and a couple of beers to ease the hangover. The day had been a struggle, but the work had been completed, and that made it all worthwhile.

On the way home he decided to stop at a small store on East Vista Way to buy a six-pack of beer. Early in the day he had made a promise to himself to make changes in his life and he was ready to test his new-found discipline by only drinking a couple of beers per day, instead of the customary six-pack.

He pulled the truck into the store's parking lot and parked next to a dark blue Nissan Sentra. He was busy placing some invoices together on his clipboard when he heard a familiar voice call his name.

"Hey, Francisco!"

"Hey, Chino, what's going on?" Frank was happy to see his friend again. Chino was only one of a handful of people that actually called Frank by his Spanish name.

Chino was a nickname. People called him Chino because of his long curly hair. Gonzalo Lara was twenty-eight years old and lived in a trailer inside an avocado orchard off Ormsby Street. Every now and then Chino let Frank drop a truckload of dry wood, tree branches and palm tree fronds in one of the ravines located on the north side of the avocado orchard. It saved Frank a trip to the landfill, about twenty miles away. Chino was a full-time avocado orchard manager and one of the small-time cocaine dealers in the area.

Frank placed the clipboard on the passenger side seat, pulled on the door handle and got out of the truck. With short strides he walked towards the entrance of the liquor store.

Chino was standing next to the public phone located near the entrance. Posing and wearing his trademark sunglasses and Hawaiian shirt, Chino smiled as Frank approached. When the public phone rang Chino lifted the receiver on the second ring, moved it to his ear and began to talk. Frank nodded his head towards him as a sign of greeting, and then kept walking toward the entrance of the store.

Inside the store, Frank walked to the back, opened a refrigerator door, and selected a six pack of Corona beer. He walked to the counter, and paid for the beer with a twenty dollar bill. After collecting his change, he walked out.

Outside the store, Frank opened his pack of cigarettes, took one out, and stopped to light it.

"Cerveza Corona? Hey, are you celebrating?" Chino opened his arms in mock surprise.

"Yes, I am," Frank answered with a smile on his face, taking a couple of puffs from his cigarette.

"Hey, I am also celebrating," Chino added with a smile on his face.

"What's happening?" Frank was genuinely curious.

Chino removed his sunglasses, placed his right arm around Frank's shoulders, and steered Frank towards his truck.

"I have finally made a connection with the big boys. I'm finally connected. Do you know what I mean?"

"No, Chino, I don't know what you mean," Frank replied, feeling uneasy.

"I am not dealing with small change anymore. I know people with lots of money and lots of kilos." Chino began to smile again.

"Jesus, Chino. That crap is not a game, it's dangerous. You got to be careful with those guys." Frank's smile faded.

With a serious look on his face, Chino leaned closer to Frank and said, "I know what you mean, but I want lots of money. And I am not stupid, because I know I will work hard for the money."

"Come on Chino, you make it sound like there is a pile of money and all you have to do is pick it up and throw it in the trunk of your car and then deliver it to your friends."

Frank was beginning to get uncomfortable with his friend and with the conversation.

"Hey, I sell cocaine but I do not mix business with pleasure. Cocaine is for people stupid enough to buy it. Besides, I have serious protection against those guys." Chino was trying to smile, hoping to lower the tension that was beginning to rise.

"What, do you have your own personal bodyguards?" Frank said smiling.

Chino looked at Frank and then shook his head. "No bodyguards. I have something better, much better." He got closer to Frank and almost whispered in his ear, "I have tapes with names and phone numbers. If something happens to me . . ."

"Shit, Chino!" Frank pulled away from Chino, as if he was trying to avoid catching germs from a deleterious disease.

"Those tapes with names and other crap like that can get you killed." Frank pulled the truck's keys out and selected the ignition key. He wanted to get the hell away; he was afraid someone might be watching and assume he was Chino's cocaine partner.

"I am only saying this to you because you are my best friend and—"

"Jesus, Chino. Please don't tell me—I honestly don't want to know anything." Frank opened the door and got inside the truck.

Chino continued with the conversation, "Don't worry, the next time you see me, I will have a new car and lots of money."

"I don't know." He paused. "But you are a big boy, Chino." Frank let out a sigh as he started the truck.

Before pulling away Frank remembered he needed to collect the receipts he dropped with the truckload of dry wood and palm tree fronds in the back area of the avocado orchard the last time he stopped by to visit Chino.

"Speaking of money, the last time I was at your place I lost some receipts."

"You lost what?" Chino answered with a confused look on his face.

"I lost papers and some receipts. I need to find them so that I can get my money back. I think I lost them when I dropped the truckload of wood material at your place early this week. Are you going to be home later?"

"Yes, but not for long," Chino began to put on his sunglasses.

"I'm going to my place to take a shower and then I'll be right over. OK?" Frank said.

"I have a meeting with some people tonight. Just come and get your papers or whatever you need," Chino replied.

Chino was in good spirits; after years of selling nickel and dime bags, patience and smarts finally had paid off. Chino had secured an interview, a meeting of sorts, with a group of American and Mexican cocaine dealers working out of the Mesa de Otay Border area in Tijuana. Chino was not a fool; he was aware of the risks and consequences the drug business produced, primarily the torture and violent death at the hands of drug thugs and police officers from Tijuana.

According to the Gospel of Chino, the key to success was to do your job well and stay low key. Chino felt self-confident because there was an insurance policy in his possession. Safely hidden away at home was a set of computer floppy disks with information related to border agents from the Temecula and Otay Mesa/Mesa de Otay Border check points and federal officers from downtown San Diego. The computer floppy disks had been a gift from Mario, a fellow drug dealer he had known for years from Oceanside, the military city connected to Camp Pendleton, a Marine Base located thirty-eight miles north of San Diego.

One particular day after drinking a few beers and snorting lines of cocaine, Mario bragged about being part of a sophisticated group of American agents and Mexican people moving drugs across the border on a regular basis. One night after two days of heavy partying, Mario overdosed on cocaine and heroin, but before his death Mario had asked Chino to keep the computer floppy disks in a safe place.

After Mario's death, Chino spread the word he was available for the vacancy left by his friend, and at one point he offered cocaine and money in exchange for a name or a phone number of a person or persons that could help him join Mario's organization.

Nothing happened.

After months of chasing leads, Chino decided to use common sense, and stop making noise, and just wait for somebody to make the first move.

It was a smart decision.

Within a month somebody texted him the phone number of a pay phone in National City. From a payphone he called the phone number in National City and was told to be at a restaurant in Tijuana on the 15th at 8:00 p.m. The restaurant was located within walking distance from the Otay Mesa-Mesa de Otay Border crossing.

Frank placed the truck in reverse, pulled out of the parking stall and then slowly moved forward. He stopped to check for traffic at the end of the parking lot and then headed west on East Vista Way.

A couple of miles later he turned north on Taylor Lane and less than a mile he made a right turn and got on a private gravel road. The truck moved along until it reached the oak tree in front of his trailer. Frank turned off the truck's engine and just sat there. He reached for one of the beers, and twisted off the cap with his right hand. Frank took a long swallow of the beer, placed the bottle between his legs and stared at the trailer.

After John's speech, Frank decided to make drastic changes, physically and mentally. After another swallow the bottle was returned to its cardboard container.

Frank looked intently at the front of the trailer, his mind lost in thought.

Ten years ago life was good; he was thirty-five years old, single and with a small construction business. In the beginning, work was slow, but within two years he had made enough to buy this trailer. He met his wife Rebecca at the local bank one Monday morning. Rebecca was the bank's assistant manager and had the most beautiful smile he had ever seen in his life. He fell in love with her long brown hair and light brown eyes.

For two years Rebecca and Frank worked long hours. Their goal was to build a home, have a family and live happily ever after. But work slowed to a crawl. Instead of changing business tactics, Frank blamed other businesses for his misfortunes. At first Frank started to drink out of frustration. He drank because he got a good deal, or because he lost a good contract. Later he didn't need an excuse. One night after one of his regular beer drinking sessions, he came home to an empty trailer.

Rebecca was gone and he didn't have the courage to go after her.

One Friday night while drinking beer at a local bar, a migrant worker named Raul asked him for a ride to his camp. It was getting late and somehow he had missed his ride back to his place. Raul lived with seven other workers in a trailer owned by their employer, a local nurseryman.

The migrant worker told him there was beer and American girls at his camp, but if he wanted some sex he had to pay for it. Frank gave Raul a ride back to the camp and decided to stay for a while. At the camp groups of workers drank beer and talked about their hometowns, their girlfriends, their wives and kids. Many had left their homes to travel north to start a new life; others sent money home to support their families and pay debts; a few left for the adventure. Most of the migrant workers kept out of sight and lived in camps with only the bare necessities.

A girl named Julia was there. She was tall, thin and extremely good looking. Chino was with her; Frank had met Chino years ago at a construction site in Fallbrook. Frank had been hired to install the landscaping and build the patio covers for the five model homes of *Las Brisas*, the newest project of the Finite Construction Company of San Diego. Chino sold beer to the day-laborers everyday of the week. Every now and then Frank bought a beer from Chino. Then it became a routine to buy a beer and listen to Chino's plans to make money selling beer and other products to the labor force. Chino had come from Maniadero, a town south of Ensenada, in Baja California, in his late teens, and had planned to retire by his thirty-fifth birthday. When the model homes had been completed Frank told Chino about other construction sites in the area. Chino was grateful for the information. Later, Chino expanded his business. He became a businessman appreciated by day-laborers and migrant workers because he brought joy and happiness to those that had dollars in their pockets. Chino arrived at migrant camps ready to wheel and deal. With three or four girls in tow, usually high on drugs, he instructed the clientele to form a line and to have their money ready.

That Friday night a line of migrant workers waited their turn outside homemade shacks and small trailers. Forty dollars bought each migrant worker waiting in line ten minutes worth of happiness.

Alcohol gave Frank the courage to invite Julia to have a beer with him back in his trailer. To his surprise, she accepted. Once they got to the trailer, he was embarrassed about the condition of the living room. He tried to clean and apologize for the mess, but she didn't seem to mind. She walked to the bedroom and sat on the floor in front of the bed with her legs crossed.

Frank opened the refrigerator door and got two beers and gave her one. She opened her beer, took one sip and then placed the bottle on the floor next to the wall. Then she pulled a plastic bag of cocaine from her purse. Frank sat on the floor in front of her. He was only a beer drinker, but was too proud and stupid to admit he was not a cocaine user. Most people he knew had tried it, except him. But he wanted to impress Julia. He snorted a couple of cocaine lines with her and tried to make small talk.

Frank wanted to ask how a girl like her became friends with a guy like Chino, but he knew better. She would probably be insulted and leave. He looked at Julia and started to laugh nervously. As the cocaine started to take effect he felt wide awake, as if the night had turned into day. Aided by the rush of cocaine he moved closer to Julia. God, she was beautiful.

Frank touched her hair and held some of it in his hand. Her hair smelled like expensive soap. Julia didn't move or say anything. She placed the plastic bag inside her purse and then placed the purse next to the beer bottle. Frank grabbed her face with both of his hands and kissed her lightly. Julia just closed her eyes. Her face and neck had the scent of gardenias. He kissed her again, slowly, and she kissed him back.

The rest was a blur.

He remembers leaning back, placing his head against the foot of the bed for a few seconds, closing his eyes to rest. When he opened his eyes again, it was daylight.

Julia was gone.

He put his pants back on and threw himself on the bed and slept for the rest of the day. That episode seemed like a lifetime ago.

A dog barking in the distance brought Frank back from his daydream.

Frank remembered the mess in the kitchen and in the bedroom. He gathered the six-pack of beer, the pack of cigarettes, got out of the truck and, walked towards the front door of the trailer. He decided to clean his trailer first. Driving to Chino's place to collect the receipts would have to wait until Sunday or Monday. It didn't matter; there was plenty of time.

Frank placed the beer inside the refrigerator and with his newfound willpower, he went to work. The trailer was cleaned from top to bottom, different types of trash sorted out, bagged and placed outside the trailer, ready to be taken to the landfill. A much needed list of groceries was made and posted on the refrigerator door. By the time all the household tasks were completed, it was dark outside.

After washing the last set of dishes Frank moved towards the bathroom to take a bath. The bath was set hotter than normal. Before the bathtub got full Frank removed his clothes and slowly got inside the tub. The water was hot but once he sat inside the bathtub and found a comfortable position, the water felt good. Frank wanted the hot water to remove all the terrible thoughts he felt at that moment and to wash away years of guilt and sad memories.

Four

La Parrilla Restaurant
Otay Mesa-Mesa de Otay, Tijuana,
Baja California
Saturday December 19, 2009

Chino was nervous as hell. After waiting for years for a chance to make money selling drugs across the border, the opportunity had arrived. But was he ready to play with the "big boys"? Chino was not sure. The bravado he had demonstrated earlier in the day for the benefit of Frank had long ago evaporated.

In order to avoid the Saturday afternoon traffic along the freeways that led to the Otay Mesa Border checkpoint, Chino left his trailer two hours early. He crossed the border without delay and with plenty of time to spare. Five short blocks after crossing the border he found the meeting place, a family diner named *La Parrilla* Restaurant.

Taking his time, Chino drove past the eating place without turning and looking at the people moving along the sidewalk. He was early for his appointment and he didn't know what else to do. Two blocks later he made a u-turn and unhurriedly drove back until he found a parking space across the street from the restaurant, next to a local park. The street lights illuminated the concrete benches facing the street while the park's fluorescent lights lit up the concrete pathways where toddlers and older kids walked under the careful supervision of their parents.

After turning the engine off Chino sat there thinking, wondering if he had made the correct decision by accepting the invitation to this meeting. Before tonight, dealing in small quantities of drugs was tantalizing, but right now his stomach was full of butterflies and bile was forming in his mouth.

With hesitation, he got out of his car and tentatively crossed the street, avoiding cars going by and pedestrians milling about.

Chino found a table in the middle of the restaurant and sat facing the street. The other tables in the restaurant were occupied by couples and families, all enjoying a Saturday evening meal. *Ranchero* music was coming out of speakers hanging from the back wall, but most customers were too engrossed in their own conversations to notice it.

When a young waiter approached the table, Chino told him he was waiting for more people to join him. The waiter nodded and graciously departed to help other customers. With an attentive look on his face, Chino surveyed the customers inside the restaurant, hoping to notice something unusual, but it was a waste of time because he really didn't know what to look for. Outside the restaurant, single people, couples and families with their kids walked by.

Eight o'clock came and went, and nobody came to join him at his table.

This is a test. Be patient, he told himself.

At 8:30 p.m., approaching from the left side of the street, an American and a Mexican entered the restaurant and moved directly to Chino's table, and without preamble, the American took a seat, while the Mexican moved past them and sat at a table against the wall, facing the street.

Apparently they knew Chino.

The American sitting to the right of Chino was tall, had short gray hair and an air of arrogance. He wore a dark blue sports jacket, jeans and dark New Balance running shoes. The Mexican sitting by the wall had a semi-dark complexion, brown hair and wore a dark brown leather jacket, jeans and cowboy boots.

When the young waiter returned to the table to take their order, Chino declined but the American ordered a Dos Equis beer. While they waited, Chino turned to look at the Mexican sitting at the table behind them. The Mexican didn't look back; he concentrated on the clientele inside the restaurant. A couple of minutes later the waiter brought a Dos Equis beer and placed it on the table.

The American took a long swallow of the beer and shifted in his chair trying to find a comfortable position. He looked inattentive, almost bored.

Chino concentrated on the pedestrians walking past the restaurant.

"Sabes hablar Ingles?" The American asked Chino.

Chino nodded his head instead of answering. A move he immediately regretted.

"OK, Chino man, I understand you are looking for a job?" The American continued.

Chino didn't know what to say.

"Well?" The American said, waiting for an answer.

"I want to make money," Chino replied, turning and looking the American straight in the eyes.

"You make it sound simple and this is not an easy business," the American responded.

"I'm only being honest," Chino answered.

"Let's cut the bullshit and get to the point," the American said, annoyed. "All right, if you want the job, it's yours." The American paused for a few seconds to take another long swallow of beer.

"First, you must follow some rules. If you get arrested and sent to jail, you are fucked, because I don't care. Second, you do what I say, period. And last, under no circumstances are you allowed to give names or information related to our group to anybody, unless I tell you." He paused again to take another swallow of his beer and then added, "Do you understand?"

"Yes," Chino answered without conviction.

"Do you have any questions for me?" The American asked.

"No," Chino replied quickly. The interview had lost its appeal and Chino wanted to get out of the restaurant as fast as possible.

"Are you fucking sure?" the American asked again, pausing to finish his beer. After placing the empty bottle down, he leaned across the table, and in a flat voice said, "Right now somebody is checking your car from top to bottom, and if we find something suspicious, something strange, you are fucked. So if you have anything to say, now is the time."

"No," Chino replied again with no emotion.

"Good," the American said. He raised his hand and asked the waiter for another beer.

"Just relax for a few minutes." He pushed his chair away from his table and then crossed his legs. The waiter brought the beer and the American grabbed the bottle and took a long swallow.

For the next few minutes neither one made a comment; the American was content to enjoy his beer in silence. Minutes later a person walked in and came to Chino's table. He leaned next to the American, and whispered something in his ear. The American's face did not change expression, he only nodded in affirmation. Once the message was delivered the man stood up and walked away.

"Well, so far so good," the American said, beginning to smile. After taking another sip of beer he said, "One last question, but take your time before you answer. Just think about the question, OK?"

"OK," Chino answered in a barely audible voice.

"Did your friend Mario give you any information, like papers, notes with phone numbers, or names of people for you to keep?"

"No," Chino answered right away. Even though he had expected the question and had practiced the answer many times at home, the question caught him off guard. He was beginning to perspire under his shirt; his confidence was beginning to erode.

Keep your cool! He kept repeating to himself.

Turning and looking at the table behind them he noticed the Mexican was smoking. For a split second he wanted to ask for a cigarette, not because he craved the nicotine, but because he wanted something to do with his hands. He decided against it; his actions could be misinterpreted.

"Mario was a good man, but unfortunately, he was also fucking stupid. He was holding out on us. He got greedy and then started to use drugs," the American said matter-of-factly.

"This is a business. You follow the rules and you are fine. You screw up, you pay the price, just like your friend Mario." The American took a long swallow of his beer, finished it, and placed it next to the other empty one.

The American looked at Chino and said, "Don't fucking lie to me. Ever." He pointed with his finger at Chino as if it was a gun. He held the finger for a couple of seconds and then placed his hands back on the table. Chino understood the message, nodded and said, "OK."

"All right, here's the deal. You are to call a phone number every other Monday at eight o'clock in the morning, right on the dot. If you don't call, I have to assume something awful happened, like you are dead or in jail. So you better have a fucking good excuse for not calling. Once you call you'll get instructions on what to do."

The American placed a small piece of paper on the table. "Look at the phone number on the paper, memorize it and then destroy it. Do it before you leave this place."

"OK," Chino answered, looking at the paper.

"Your first call is a week from this coming Monday," the American added.

"OK," Chino said again.

"Good," the American said. Then he added, "Be at your place tomorrow. We are going to stop by and say hello. Don't go anywhere." Not waiting for an answer he pulled his chair away from his table and got up. He nodded to the Mexican sitting at the other table and then pointed to Chino and said, "Don't fuck up."

The American pushed his chair close to the table, took a twenty-dollar bill from his front pocket and put it down on the table, and headed toward the front door.

The Mexican waited a couple of minutes before exiting the restaurant. Chino sat still, his brain racing a hundred miles an hour, trying to figure out what was going on. He picked up the paper from the table, looked at the phone number written on it, closed his eyes and did his best to memorize it. He read the numbers again and again. Leaning his head forward as in prayer, he closed his eyes for a few seconds, doing his best to remember the phone number. When he felt sure the numbers were familiar, he ripped the paper into small pieces.

With hesitation Chino got up, pushed the chair back against the table and stood there for a couple of seconds, contemplating his options. His heart was beating fast. He was hoping not to find unpleasant surprises outside the restaurant. At the door of the restaurant he looked both ways before crossing the street.

Before Chino got to his car he reached into his pocket and pulled out his car keys. His hands were shaking and he was beginning to sweat even though the night was cool. When he got to his car he inserted the key and unlocked the door. The only noise was the click of the car being unlocked but no explosion. He opened the door of the car and got in.

Taking a deep breath, Chino leaned against the steering wheel, inserted the key into the ignition switch, closed his eyes, and turned the key to start the car. The engine came to life with a loud roar, startling Chino; he pulled his hand away from the ignition switch so fast it hit part of the steering wheel.

"Shit!" Chino yelled, leaning back against the car seat. It took him a few seconds to catch his breath. He looked towards the restaurant. Nobody was coming after him. After regaining his composure he pulled the car out of the parking space and drove to the end of the street. At the corner he made a left turn and then headed straight for the Otay Mesa-Mesa de Otay Border crossing.

Five

Restaurante La Tortuga
Playas de Rosarito, Baja California
Sunday December 20, 2009

Javier and David met for an early breakfast at *La Tortuga* Restaurant. Both did their best to steer the conversation away from the business at hand: crossing the border in twenty-four hours, apprehending American citizens and returning with them to Rosarito.

What's the big deal about that?

David was the first to address the issue. He took a sip of coffee, and then placed the cup gingerly back on the saucer.

"I have been meaning to say something about the investigation for a long time. I even wrote notes down on a piece of paper to make sure I shared with you the details I felt were important. Each time I tried, however, the timing was not right or we lacked one piece of information."

Javier remained quiet.

"Five years ago when we met to talk about the murder of Luis and Ramiro, I was flattered, like a kid, a fifth grader who's been asked to join the high school varsity team. But then reality set in. I was at my mother's house trying to ease her fears about me dying in a shootout with a group of local *narcotraficantes* or getting caught in the crossfire between crooked police officers, when it hit me: my mother thought, or I had given her the impression, that I had all the qualities of a well-trained federal agent. I said to myself, who the hell am I? I'm not a well-trained, sophisticated character from a Robert Ludlum novel, like Jason Bourne or one of those analytical agents that solve crimes in 48 hours in television shows like "Law and Order". I am just a local police officer with some training with the San Diego Police Department, doing my best to impress the federal agency here in Baja. And nothing else."

He stopped to take a sip of his coffee. The coffee was lukewarm, and was beginning to lose its flavor.

"After I left my mother's house I went to visit my sister. Then more doubts began to creep in. I felt useless, incompetent. It took days to feel better, to regain my confidence. Yesterday after we had the meeting with Manny I went to visit my mother and sister. At home I had a long conversation with my girlfriend, and then took a nap. I was tired. When I got up I took a hot shower, and as I dried myself, I framed a picture of the investigation. Four years ago, after we got a hold of the first clue, I had a sense that we could actually find the killers. And you know what? We did. But yesterday, after Manny gave us the information, I considered crossing the border into San Ysidro, arresting the banker and the federal officers in San Diego, and then coming back to Rosarito alive, to docking at the space station orbiting the earth without the need of the Space Shuttle."

David reached for a napkin to wipe his lips, more out of reflex than need.

"Now let me tell you something," David continued, his voice was animated and his brown eyes had acquired a brighter shine.

"As we sit here this morning I am confident we can drive north of the border, get the job done, and come out of this alive. I don't have evidence, only a gut feeling. My family believes this is a suicide mission, and maybe it is. Who knows? But deep down I know we are coming back home to our families. I don't intend to die someplace else. I've been with you for the last five years and I'm not backing down now; I intend to complete the task, despite the consequences."

A faint grin was painted on David's face.

It was Javier's turn. The last five years had been a physical, emotional and spiritual roller coaster for both of them. Javier did his best to hold back his emotions but couldn't; tears started to form.

Five years ago out of desperation he had asked David to help him find the killers of his cousin Luis Hernandez and his friend Ramiro Flores because he didn't have anybody else to turn to. He went to David for help but in reality he was asking David and his family to place their lives in danger for the benefit of the Hernandez and Flores families, and he knew he hadn't earned the right to ask for so much.

But he was desperate.

Their odyssey lasted five years, and in that time they had become more than brothers-in-arms, and more than family. Both had secrets their families didn't know about and both had promised to safeguard each other's families in case one of them didn't make it to the end.

Javier got up, went into the kitchen and grabbed a white towel from a rack, passed a portion of it through the warm water faucet, washed his face and came back to the table.

Out of respect David remained quiet.

After composing himself, Javier explained, "I have three situations, and you can give me your feelings on each. First, we arrest them, bring them back and then let the Rosarito police take it from there. Second, we arrest them and turn them over to the San Diego Police."

Javier waited a few seconds before continuing. "The third option is about making things right. They have blood on their hands and I don't want to bring them back alive. We arrest them, and between San Diego and Tijuana we get rid of them."

David nodded and said, "I have no problem with that."

"I did my best yesterday to come up with ideas, but there is not much to plan. We drive to National City to get the car, and we find Thomas. He will lead us to the other two guys."

"Do we have a backup plan?" David asked, with an interrogating look on his face.

Javier looked down at his coffee cup. After a couple of seconds he said, "I don't have a plan in case we can't arrest them, or if the situation gets out of control, or if we get caught."

"Good. It means we can't fail," David said smiling.

Looking out the window and into the distance Javier said, "I want to spend the rest of the day with my family. Unless you think otherwise, I want to cross the border tomorrow early in the morning."

David simply said, "I'll be ready."

Six

Vista, California
Sunday December 20, 2009

Frank's new lifestyle was still going strong twenty-four hours later. A constructive attitude made it possible to have a productive Sunday morning and afternoon.

The alarm went off at 7:00 a.m. and for the first time in years Frank saw the light of day cutting across the bedroom window without a taste of bile in his mouth and a pounding headache. After a hot shower in a white, glowingly clean bathtub, he went to the small kitchen and cooked himself a vegetable omelet.

After eating his breakfast Frank did more cleaning. Broken appliances, old kitchen utensils, worn-out clothes were placed in cardboard boxes, while all the work-related papers and old receipts were shredded and placed in plastic trash bags. The paperwork related to the last two jobs was sorted out. The receipts for each residence had been neatly tabulated and placed in two separate folders; the only items missing were the receipts he dropped at Chino's place when he unloaded dry tree branches in the avocado orchard's ravine days ago.

In the late afternoon Frank drove the four-mile distance to Chino's place, located in an avocado orchard, at Ormsby Street and East Vista Way. It was still light when Frank got to the orchard. The orchard was almost sixty square acres, with a trailer at the entrance; near the middle of the land was an open area with three large ravines. Frank entered the orchard using the East Vista Way entrance, parked his truck near one of the ravines, put his work gloves on, and sorted out the dry material into bundles of tree branches and palm fronds. After ten minutes of rummaging, Frank found the yellow-colored invoices he was looking for. By then the sun was descending on the nearby hills.

Placing the work gloves away, he neatly folded the invoices and placed them in his shirt pocket. Frank gazed in the direction of Chino's trailer, tucked inside thick, green rows of avocado trees. Frank didn't bother to stop by and say hello because Sunday was Chino's day off. He was probably away someplace, enjoying a beer and hanging out with his new friends, the "heavy hitters" from south of the border. Frank had no time to socialize, he just wanted to find the receipts and go home to complete the paperwork.

When Frank turned towards his truck he noticed the mountains to the east and he couldn't help being mesmerized by the gorgeous pale-yellow sunlight flooding the green trees and plants; it was a stunning sight.

The noise of dry branches breaking behind him startled him. On instinct Frank made a quick turn, bumping into a large flashlight that was pointed at his chest. Frank was caught off-guard; he was so engrossed looking at the sunlight bathing the mountains he hadn't heard anybody coming.

A man holding the large flashlight said, "Who the hell are you and what are you looking for?" The man was tall, heavy set, sweaty, wearing worn-out jeans, a faded green T-shirt and a ponytail.

The man pushed the flashlight against Frank's chest with force.

"Go to hell, I am not telling you anything!" Frank responded, more out of fear than boldness. With his right hand he pushed the flashlight away from his chest. The flashlight felt heavy.

"Give me an answer! Who are you and what are you looking for?" the man with the flashlight asked again.

Behind the heavyset man, standing near a row of avocado trees, about eighty feet away, Frank could distinguish three silhouettes.

Who are these people?

"His name is Frank and he is my friend, please leave him alone." The voice came out slow and timid.

Was that Chino? Frank didn't know what to do or how to respond. He stood there, looking at the silhouettes and at the sweaty guy, waiting for something to happen.

The silhouettes moved forward towards the guy with the flashlight. In the group was a tall, older guy with gray hair, Chino and Julia, the girl he had met before. Chino stood still, arms to the side, with no expression on his face. Julia was pale, nervous, her fingers twitching and her hair was disheveled.

What the hell? Frank knew something was wrong and it had to do with Chino and his stupid drug dealing.

"Look, I don't know what's going on and I don't care. I'm done here and I just want to go home" Frank was trying to sound disinterested; not afraid, yet, not courageous either. "I came to find some papers I lost earlier this week. I have found them, and like I said, I'm going home."

Frank took the receipts from his shirt pocket and waved them to the group. He turned around and started to walk away. Frank's steps were short and slow. It felt like an eternity getting to his truck. Frank was certain somebody was going to call his name or tell him to stop.

Nothing happened.

Still rattled from the meeting with the sweaty guy with the flashlight and the rest of the group, Frank got into his truck and sped away.

Seven

San Diego, California
Monday December 21, 2009

Javier and David crossed the San Ysidro Border checkpoint without delay; they were part of thousands of commuters crossing the border each day. Both had local passports which entitled them to visit San Diego County for three days without the need of a visa. Another officer from Rosarito delivered them to an address in National City, located fifteen minutes north of San Ysidro.

After a pleasant drive north along the 805 Freeway, the driver took the Plaza Boulevard exit, made a right turn on Highland Avenue, and dropped David and Javier at the corner of 4th Street and Kenton Avenue in National City. David and Javier walked north along Kenton Avenue for one block until they found the Mendez's house. The vehicle Manny described was in the back of the house, parked in the alley. It was a wine colored 1989 Volvo 240 DL.

While David kept an eye on the alley, Javier opened the trunk and checked the contents inside. The car had a new spare tire; the tire jack was almost new; a new red one-gallon gasoline container was full; a box of 50 gallon trash bags was next to a ziplock bag containing latex gloves; two pairs of leather work gloves; two baseball caps with San Diego logos on them; a Ziploc storage bag with white plastic zip ties was placed next to three rolls of duct tape; and two 60-inch pieces of nylon rope.

Manny had thought of everything.

Javier reached in and checked beneath the spare tire. He found a thick bundle. After unrolling a large piece of heavy cloth, two nine-millimeter guns with two boxes of bullets came into view. He returned the weapons and closed the trunk.

He unlocked the car on the driver's side and got in. David got in the passenger's seat. Before starting the engine, he glanced over the chain link fence towards the house. Someone was pulling the window curtains aside. It was Beatriz Mendez, his aunt. She smiled at him and he smiled back. Javier adjusted the rear view mirror before starting the engine. It was the point of no return. Javier glanced at David and David just nodded in affirmation, his face looking straight ahead.

The car exited the alley and moved south two blocks and when they got to Fourth Street, made a right turn and drove west for four blocks until Javier saw the ramp leading to the North 5 Freeway. The car got on the freeway and headed north along the coast towards Encinitas. As the car moved along the freeway, Javier couldn't help but wonder how his life would have been different if his parents had not died in that terrible accident so long ago.

Eight

Ensenada, Baja California
December, 1970

At three o'clock on a Sunday morning, driving along the main street of Ensenada, Carlos, a Rosarito police officer and Adela Ortega, an elementary school teacher, were in high spirits, the songs from the orchestra and mariachi bands still resonating in their minds. A simple but traditional wedding ceremony of the youngest daughter of a fellow police officer had been a success.

The ceremony was held at *La Iglesia de Santa Maria,* a small church located in the heart of the city. The one-hour wedding mass had started at two o'clock in the afternoon and, to the delight of friends and acquaintances, it ended exactly one hour and thirty-five minutes later, a rarity for a Mexican wedding.

The reception had been scheduled at five in

the afternoon, followed by dinner and then the customary money dance, none starting or ending at the prescribed time. Throughout the evening Carlos and Adela had ample time to meet new people, and to reacquaint themselves with old ones.

After a fine meal and hours of dancing to popular and romantic music of the 1950s and 1960s, performed by an 18-piece orchestra, a mariachi band and a DJ, Carlos and Adela decided to call it a night. Sometime before three o'clock in the morning the Ortegas walked along the rows of tables surrounding the dancing floor and approached the newlyweds and wished them life-long happiness, and to the families of the bride and groom, they expressed sincere thanks for the invitation to a wonderful wedding ceremony.

The Ortegas also stopped by to say goodbye to other police members and their families from Rosarito and Ensenada and to old friends. When their car pulled out of the parking lot they could still hear the mariachi band playing and the crowd singing along to a romantic song. The Ortegas were heading north, back to their home in Rosarito, a forty-five minute drive from Ensenada.

Along the main avenue, traffic noise, music blaring from the bars, clatter from tourists and locals walking about gave Ensenada a festive mood. Carlos rolled down the window to enjoy the fresh air. As the car moved along the narrow streets, Carlos and Adela talked about the growth of the city and the fascination of tourists with the town of Ensenada. The Ortegas left the downtown area driving away from the city, towards State Highway 1.

At the north entrance of town, an eighteen-wheel flat-bed construction truck, hauling 20-kilo bags of Tolteca Cement, veered off the two-lane boulevard and crossed the ten-inch concrete divider. The heavy vehicle continued to drive erratically on the wrong side of the avenue, while the frantic driver was doing his best to regain control of the truck. Driving along the boulevard, distracted by the conversation, Carlos and Adela didn't notice the heavy truck moving out of control, blocking the two lanes of the boulevard at a forty-five degree angle. By the time Carlos noticed the front grill of the heavy truck rapidly approaching, he couldn't steer the car away from the trailer.

The impact of the crash sheered off the top of their vehicle, embedding the car under the frame of the trailer, dragging it for many yards. By the time the heavy truck came to a stop, ripped concrete bags and concrete powder laid scattered across the two lanes of the boulevard. Shreds of metal and plastic from the small car rolled and skidded for many yards.

Carlos and Adela died at the scene. The driver of the eighteen-wheel truck had been driving for twenty-four hours without rest and was legally drunk at the time of the crash.

When the news of the deaths of Carlos and Adela reached the town of Rosarito, police officers, friends and family members couldn't believe the irony of the misfortune: The Ortegas didn't drink or smoke and Carlos had no tolerance for those who drank themselves into a stupor and then got behind the wheel of a car. It was common practice for friends and family members and police officers to be indifferent when friends and neighbors got behind the wheel of a car after drinking more than a few beers, placing innocent bystanders in danger. For years Carlos Ortega had fought against the heavy drinking culture of his community and his fellow officers in the Rosarito Police Department.

Friends, family members and police officers from Rosarito, Tijuana and Ensenada came to the funeral to pay their respects to the Ortega Family.

The families of Carlos and Adela Ortega met at *La Tortuga* Restaurant to decide the fate of a shy thirteen-year-old boy named Javier, the Ortega's only son.

After much deliberation Javier was placed with the Hernandez family. Florentino Hernandez was Adela's older brother and a police officer. Genoveva Hernandez was a homemaker and a community activist. The Hernandez family lived in a modest home with their nineteen-year-old son, Luis and their pet dog.

While the conferences were taking place Javier stayed at his parents' home, closely guarded by his grandmother. During the proceedings, nobody asked Javier what he wanted. At that moment he felt lost, abandoned and betrayed by the almighty God for taking away his parents in a senseless accident.

Javier accepted the decision to live with the Hernandez family with apprehension; other than a family reunion or a birthday party, Javier didn't have opportunities to create family ties with members outside his parents and grandparents.

Javier was alone in the world, an outsider looking in. He was a thirteen-year-old boy forced to earn a place in a household full of strangers.

Despite the initial fear, an emotional connection began to materialize with his adoptive family. The psychological and spiritual wounds began to heal. Javier smiled again. He began to talk about his parents and childhood memories. The Hernandez family provided Javier the emotional stability he desperately needed. In return, Javier gave Florentino and Genoveva the second son they wanted, but for medical reasons, couldn't have.

A key factor to Javier's emotional stability was Luis. Despite a six-year difference in age, Luis never made Javier feel unwanted at home, or in the presence of his friends. Javier was not introduced as a cousin. Luis always said, *"Este es mi Javier,"* this is my own flesh and blood. On Tuesday evenings Luis and Javier walked to the local movie theater to watch a foreign movie and afterwards get an ice cream and critique the actors. The conversations then veered to music and local politics.

Javier always felt tall around his cousin.

On Saturdays Luis played his customary *fútbol* game for a local team. On Sundays friends and family gathered to watch their favorite *fútbol* team play on television.

At twenty-five, Luis Hernandez graduated from the Universidad Autonoma de Baja California, in Ensenada. To the surprise of everyone, Luis decided to become a local policeman like his father. Rosarito police officers didn't chase bank robbers, detain famous drug dealers or mingle with federal agents from the United States. The duties included domestic disputes, controlling rowdy tourists, directing traffic, dealing with drunk drivers and writing traffic citations.

The police salary was a sensitive subject. The pay was low and rookies had to buy their uniforms, guns and ammunition. The unwritten rule was: a policeman can supplement his income in any form he deemed fit, provided he never got caught. Money was not an issue for Luis. He wanted to be a police officer because people respected him and he knew he could make a difference in his community.

One year later Luis received his police badge. The same year Luis found Teresa, the girl he always wanted, and got married. He fathered two children in the first four years of marriage. With strong dedication he immersed himself in the local community; he held monthly meetings for the families in his neighborhood and brought their concerns to city hall. At work he wrote traffic citations for moving violations and drunk drivers were thrown in jail—no free passes.

Javier started out differently. After high school Javier used his trust fund to pay the tuition at San Diego State University, in San Diego, California. Five years later he earned a degree in European literature. Family members pushed Javier to start his life in the United States; being bilingual increased the job opportunities anywhere in California.

Javier had his own plans. He became a municipal police officer like his father, uncle and cousin. Using money from his trust account and with a college friend as a partner, a small private school was created, geared towards high school students willing to master the English language.

At a family gathering he met Angelica, a middle school teacher. They dated for a year, became engaged and six months later got married. A year after, a baby girl was born. Life was good. Angelica wanted to stay home and he was satisfied being a police officer and teacher.

Angelica made it clear; she was worried about her husband being a policeman. A violent era had arrived with drug traffickers shooting each other in broad daylight and with bodies being dumped on the side of the main road. Dead bodies with missing limbs were not unusual. Television reports and newspaper articles of violent deaths of policemen helped Angelica support her position. Javier knew his wife had a point. The times were changing.

Nine

In the spring of 2003, Luis went camping for a three-day weekend at a local beach with his childhood friend and fellow police officer, Ramiro Flores. Twice a year Teresa allowed her husband to get away from the complaints of friends and neighbors about the lack of trash collection, the potholes and the illegal drag-racing, issues related to the city hall office, not to the police.

Javier and his companions only went camping to Punta Bandera, Playa Lucero or Playa Encantada, all within a fifteen-mile radius from home. For the participants there was no fishing, swimming, surfing, scuba diving or other recreational activities related to sand and surf.

The main attractions were great meals, beer drinking, and long and thorough discussions about local, national and international politics. It was not unusual for other police officers to show up unannounced and join in. One particular winter outing attracted close to twenty police officers at Punta Lucero to drink beer, eat *carne asada* and fish tacos, share police stories and debate the merits of the local and state politicians.

Luis and Ramiro left Friday morning. Teresa stood on the front yard and waved good-bye as Luis's car pulled away from the curb. The car honked before making a right turn at the end of the street.

The happy campers were due back the following Sunday, in time for the noon *fútbol* match on television. Throughout the years Luis made it clear to his family, friends, and fellow officers that unless Rosarito was being invaded by aliens from outer space, or gringos from the north, he was not available for duty on Sunday afternoons.

Friday and Saturday were uneventful. Other than giving harsh warnings to locals and tourists about the danger of driving with an open container tucked between their legs, and the futile attempts at stopping drunk American teenage girls from rolling down the window of the passenger side of the car at every traffic red light, pulling their tops up and exposing their breasts to the general public along the main avenue, Javier spent both days patrolling Avenida Juarez without a serious crisis.

At the end of each day, Javier called Teresa to say hello and share some of the stories, especially the funny ones. Javier made it a point to call Teresa at home when Luis was out camping for the weekend.

On Sunday Teresa got up early, and after a light breakfast, she got ready for the ten o'clock morning mass and the usual morning phone call from her husband. But something felt off. At nine forty-five, there was no phone call. Feeling edgy, she decided to skip mass. Not knowing what else to do, she decided to be practical. She changed into a pair of jeans and a light-blue cotton blouse. She went into the kitchen, put on an apron and got busy making snacks for the *fútbol* game. She called Javier to let him know she was not going to her morning mass. Javier was surprised; the last time Teresa skipped mass was two years ago, when she had a nasty cold. He wanted to ask why she had missed church, but decided not to.

After putting the snacks away, Teresa fixed a cup of coffee, walked to the living room and found a spot on the couch. Her husband was usually punctual with his phone call to the house. Why was he late calling? She called her husband's cell phone and after five rings it went into the voice mail. After the beep, she asked him to call home.

She started to worry. Did Luis and Ramiro have car problems?

Nervous, she called Javier again. When Javier picked up the phone, she said, "Luis hasn't called me. I called his cell phone but he didn't answer. I left a message. Do you think I should send somebody to look for them?"

With a calm voice Javier responded, "Teresa, Luis can take care of himself. If they need help, they will call. Just wait." To reassure her he quickly added, "He'll be home soon. Don't worry."

In reality, neither one knew how to react; Luis always came back on time, in good spirits, ready to watch the fútbol game. Javier considered possible reasons.

Maybe a family needed help at the beach. Or a driver stranded on the frontage road and they had stopped to assist.

To calm Teresa, Javier and his family came over to keep her company and wait for Luis to come from the camping trip.

Friends and neighbors arrived at eleven-thirty and sat in their customary places. As the clock hanging on the wall ticked, the tension in the house increased. By twelve o'clock everyone was restless. The television set was on, but nobody was concentrating on the game. Teresa wanted the phone to ring and bring good news. At two o'clock the game ended. Teresa walked to the front door and leaned against the door frame. She gazed along the street, lost in thought. Where the hell are they?

At two-fifteen Javier went into the bedroom, pulled out his cell phone and called the police station. Trying to sound casual Javier talked to Raquel Benitez, the front desk officer, "Hello Raquel, this is Javier."

"Hey, Javier, how was the game?"

Ignoring her question Javier asked, "Has anybody seen Luis's truck out on *La Carretera Libre*? The guys are not back from their camping trip."

With a friendly voice Raquel replied, "As of right now, have we have nobody stranded on the frontage road."

With more determination he asked, "Can you send a patrol car to check along the frontage road and at Punta Bandera? I would go myself but I don't want to worry the family."

"No problem. I will ask a patrol car to check on them. As soon as they report back, I will call you."

"Thank you, Raquel."

Javier was puzzled. If the guys were stranded on the old road connecting Rosarito to Tijuana, they would have flagged a motorist and asked for help.

Unable to remain in one place, Teresa walked back and forth, rubbing the palms of her hands, unable to control her fear. Angelica and the neighbors remained seated; there was nothing else to do.

At three o'clock the kitchen phone rang. With great composure Javier walked to the kitchen and picked up the receiver. It was bad news. The police chief received a radio call from Punta Bandera Beach a minute ago. The patrol officers found two bodies. Luis and Ramiro were dead. Both had been beaten and shot.

Javier walked back to the living room and lied to Teresa. He told everyone there was a car crash. Both were critically hurt. The chief of police asked him to drive to Punta Bandera Beach and help the officers at the scene. Teresa was not convinced; she became hysterical. She had known all day something was wrong. If Luis was hurt she wanted to be by his side. Angelica, with help from the rest of the group, convinced her to stay home and to let the police handle the accident. Javier promised to call as soon as he reached Punta Bandera Beach.

Javier walked out of the house in a daze. He drove his truck two blocks towards Avenida Juarez. At the intersection, he made a left turn and headed north, towards Highway 1, the toll road freeway. The twenty minute drive to Punta Bandera Beach seemed like an eternity.

What the hell went wrong?

When he got near Highway 1, the truck made a left turn and drove at a high speed for eleven miles on the old Rosarito-Tijuana frontage road. At the Punta Bandera Beach exit, he got off the side road and maneuvered his truck for about a mile along a dirt road; he could see cars and police vehicles in the distance. When he arrived, Javier parked his truck next to a police vehicle.

A police officer got out of his vehicle and waited for Javier to do the same. With a grim face he approached Javier and said, "I'm sorry. I wish I could say more but I can't."

Javier didn't know what to say either. He felt awkward. He simply said, "Thank you, Manuel." Looking around he asked, "Is the forensic team here?"

The officer answered, "Not yet. They are on their way."

Javier nodded. He looked down at his hands

and noticed his fingers trembling. He made a fist, trying to control the shaking.

Fear told him to run out to the beach and find his cousin. Controlling the panic ringing in his head, he moved along the narrow dirt path. About a hundred feet from the shoreline, two small camping tents were set up. Between the tents a two-meter circle surrounded a pile of ash. The policeman guarding the area moved towards Javier and said, "We don't know what the hell happened, Javier. We are sorry." Pointing to his right he added, "The boss is here. He's doing his best to sort things out."

Javier, just stood there, lost in thought. Then he said, "Thanks, Diego." Before walking away he asked, "Diego, please let me know what they find in the tents. OK?"

"I will, don't worry," answered the officer.

The waves crashing and people talking became noticeable as he approached the shore. There was no need to search for the bodies; small crowds of people told him where to go. A group of officers kept the crowd away. It was a vulgar sight. Two bodies exposed, as if naked, for all to see. The crowd had probably contaminated the crime scene. From experience he knew the forensic team only collected the bodies. Unless it involved dignitaries, there was no need to cordon-off the crime scene and gather evidence. Javier saw his boss walking towards him. The chief of police met him a short distance from the crowd of people.

Grabbing Javier by the shoulders he said, "It's pretty bad. Looking at the footprints by the tents and the location of the bodies, it was a group. But this is a small town, Javier, and we are going to find them. I give you my word. We'll find the motherfuckers."

With a hint of a smile Javier said, "Thank you, boss." Taking a breath Javier moved around the chief of police, towards the first body.

The chief of police turned, and yelled to the policemen controlling the crowd, "Get everybody away from the beach! Tell them to get the hell away from here!"

The first body belonged to Ramiro. He laid face down, the face turned to the left, arms out. It looked as if he was digging himself away from the sand, trying to reach the tents. The skin on his arms and face had wrinkled from the prolonged contact with seawater. It had acquired a creamy, chalky color. The mouth was slightly open showing blood on his teeth. His eyes were closed; there were bruises under his eyes and left cheek. A gunshot wound was visible just above the left ear. The shirt was unbuttoned. He had no socks or shoes. Two faded small brown stains were still noticeable on the back of the shirt.

Ramiro had been shot once in the head and twice in the back.

Javier approached the body and dropped one knee. He touched Ramiro's shoulder. Ramiro had been a good friend since childhood. Standing up, he noticed the crowd getting closer. He yelled, "Get the hell away from here!" The crowd took a couple of steps back but remained attentive. Javier waved to a police officer and asked for a blanket to cover Ramiro's body. The officer quickly followed the orders.

Javier kept walking along the beach towards another group of people. From a distance he recognized the body of Luis. Pain was pulling at his chest and throat. Luis's body lay face up, parallel to the water line, head facing north. The arms were close to the body, giving the appearance of being at rest. A gunshot wound on the left temple was visible. When Javier got close he dropped to his knees. He touched the face with his right hand, slowly, gently. Luis' body did not respond; it did not move. In desperation, Javier grabbed Luis's head and shoulder, trying to bring the body back to life. His cousin, his best friend, his brother, was dead. Tears rolled down his face. Noticing the crowd he repeated, "Get the hell away!" He didn't want anybody to see his cousin like this.

Javier removed his windbreaker and used it to cover Luis' face and chest and with care, he grabbed the body of his cousin and held it tight; he was trying to protect it against any more pain and degradation.

He held the body tight and cried for a long time.

Ten

According to the initial report, cocaine was found inside the camping tents of the police officers. Two days after the bodies were found, the federal police invaded Rosarito. Search warrants were issued for Luis and Ramiro's residences. Each house was meticulously inspected for illegal drugs and cash. Each family member was questioned, including the children.

Javier became guilty by association; he was related to an alleged drug trafficker. Family members and the local community were outraged by the intrusion of the federal police. Later, they understood the political implications. The new century had produced a new breed of drug dealers. They were ruthless, well-armed and unafraid to confront the federal government. Corruption had seeped into every fiber of government, from a local municipality, to the upper echelons of the Mexican administration.

The president of Mexico had made it a priority to stamp out government and police corruption and drug trafficking. Consequently, the slightest hint of drug involvement by police officers, especially along the border, sent a red alert to the federal authorities.

The state police also got involved. In case the two officers were guilty, the governor wanted the media to depict the state police as full members of the investigation, not bystanders.

The Rosarito Police office became the command center. After a two-week investigation they released a statement. The autopsy report indicated both officers had been brutally beaten and then shot. Gunpowder found at the entrance of the wounds indicated the officers were shot at close range. According to the information, all the items related to the crime were tagged, transported to a lab, and analyzed by forensic agents. Fingerprints were sent to the national database at Mexicali, the capital of Baja California, North, for analysis and matching. The weapons and shell casings were bagged and tagged, and later sent to the federal police warehouse in Ensenada along with the cocaine.

Three weeks after the official start of the investigation the bodies of the officers were released to their families for burial, and a week later, the murder case was officially closed. The official report stated the deaths of the two officers were the result of a drug transaction gone wrong. Fueled by alcohol, the officers quarreled over a kilo of cocaine. There was a physical confrontation first, followed by gunfire. Since neither of the police officers had ties to local or national *narco-traficante* groups, there were no accomplices to track down and arrest.

The official report didn't surprise family members, the local community or the Rosarito Police officers. The report was crammed with errors. The probability of the officers shooting each other in the head simultaneously defied logic. There were no explanations for the duct tape residue on the hands and upper lips of the officers, or the signs of torture. But then again, the federal police were not known for their investigative and forensic competence.

The municipal police, on the other hand, released the statement, *"La investigacion continua,"* which meant that the case of Luis and Ramiro was open until it faded from the general public's memory.

To the families the report and the crime didn't make sense. Luis and Ramiro had no federal police authority, access to heavy weapons, police secrets, or criminal or judicial value to offer to any citizen of Rosarito, Ensenada or Tijuana. Yet, they were tortured and then killed. Why?

To place cocaine in the camping tents was a foolish play; it was an act of somebody badly informed in how to make a *narco-traficante* crime scene look real.

In Baja California, drug dealers die a violent death in plain view of the general public; in a bar, at the movies, eating at a family restaurant, driving along the street with their families, at their homes or walking down the street.

The killing of the officers occurred at the beach, a few miles away from town, and if Luis and Ramiro were tortured before being shot to death, it meant outsiders were involved. In Baja California you just don't kill somebody and leave traces of drugs to confuse the authorities. It was bullshit; that type of trick only happens in low-budget Hollywood movies—and Javier knew it.

Eleven

Once the Punta Bandera Beach investigation was sealed, the federal authorities left with less fanfare than when they arrived. Soon after, the criminal case lost its luster and became old news. Outside the local community few people cared the investigation left two families in shambles, unable to meet their basic needs.

Since the deaths had a *narco-traficante* label, Teresa inherited a miniscule widow's pension courtesy of the state of Baja California to help her with her finances. She wasn't going to hear her husband scream at the television and curse at the players during *fútbol* games, help with the heated monthly community meetings, or nag local authorities to take quick actions on street improvements on behalf of their neighbors.

Ramiro Flores, a twenty-seven year veteran of the Rosarito Police Department, left a wife and two grown sons. The Flores family was left without their role model and economic provider. Beyond covering the cost of the funeral and paying a meager amount each month, Mrs. Flores was left to navigate on her own. She had no choice but to depend on family members and friends for her survival.

Raquel Benitez, the officer at the front desk, had painstakingly made copies of the documents that landed on the chief of police's desk. She had risked her job, pension and possible incarceration. She dropped off the report late one night and days later she visited Javier at home. She was bitter, angry at her boss and some of the policemen. "Luis was a hell of a police officer and a good friend. He deserves better than a bullshit investigation and a *narco* tag."

Javier thanked her and promised to do something with the report. In turn, he asked her keep their conversation a secret. There was no need to test fate.

For the next few days he couldn't eat or sleep well. All he could think about was the senseless killings.

One night after a community meeting, Javier had a conversation with his wife. Sitting at the kitchen table Javier made a plea. "I read the report and it's bullshit. It's more than just two people killing each other over a kilo of cocaine. There is a cover up, or something else. Blaming Luis and Ramiro was the easiest way out."

Angelica closed her eyes and then pressed the palms of her hands against her face. She was tense, and drained of thought. In slow motions she began to massage her eyes. "I don't know anything about police investigations. The last few weeks have been pure hell and I don't want to talk about police matters anymore," she managed to say.

"All of us are tired but—"

"I don't want to talk about police work!" Angelica cut him off in mid-sentence. She kept rubbing her eyes. The veins on her neck became enlarged.

Javier was surprised by her reaction, but she had a point: it was late and they both were tired. "I'm sorry . . . I didn't mean to upset you. Let's go to bed."

Moving away from the table she said, "Don't take this the wrong way, but you are not a police officer. You're a teacher. Let your boss handle the investigation. He promised he'll do something about it. Let him do his job."

Javier didn't answer. He was stung by her comments. Rather than to continue and make it into an argument, he let it go. "You are right. Come on let's go to bed."

Deep down he knew she was right. He felt hurt because he needed her support and approval; instead, he got a dose of reality. Angelica gave him a reason to stop and think. If there was a police conspiracy, Javier was as good as dead. And if it was more than a cover-up . . . the family was a target.

The thought of dying kept him awake for most of the night. But he couldn't let it go. The holes in the report bothered him. Maybe a conversation with the officers guarding the tents at the beach was a good starting point. The thought of knowing something was being done dropped a load off his chest. With the idea of starting his own investigation, he drifted into sleep.

Twelve

At the beginning there was an accelerating force pushing him. He was confident and full of energy. Days later, once the emotional energy dissipated, reality set in. Finding criminals required technology, training, experience, manpower, money, and police assistance.

Javier had no authority outside Rosarito Beach and limited training as a police officer. In all his years as a police officer he never fired a shot in the line of duty, chased criminals through dark alleys, or mingled with the FBI.

How the hell was he going to find the killers?

Finding a partner became a possibility. Two people can share ideas, sift through the information faster and form a layer of protection. Javier wanted a person he could trust, somebody with more experience, and not associated with the Rosarito Police.

David Avalos came to mind. They had known each other since elementary school, and every now and then had shared a cup of coffee. David was a bachelor and also a graduate of San Diego State University. David however, had participated in a ten-week police training at the San Diego Police Academy and had taken the admittance test for the Office of the Attorney General, the *Procuraduría General de la República,* the institution belonging to the federal executive branch responsible for the investigation and prosecution of federal crimes. David was clever: He knew the risks associated with being a federal police officer; hence, his reluctance to get married.

They met for coffee one morning. Javier placed a folder on the table with a copy of the police investigation inside.

The results of the lab reports contradicted the official version. The federal police arrived, produced a report, and when the time was appropriate, they left. It was political grandstanding and the chief of police went along for the ride.

Rubbing his forehead with his right hand Javier said, "I feel like I'm losing my mind. I'm lost and confused."

David just listened.

Javier continued, "I need to find out what

happened, but I don't know what to do. My wife is right: I'm a teacher first and then a part-time policeman."

David listened to the discourse, glanced at the photos, flipped the pages but refrained from asking questions, particularly the ones that had no answers. He made a commitment to help because it was the right thing to do. Years ago when the state government offered housing to low income families, Luis used his political influence to help families in the local community qualify for a home loan. Thanks to Luis, the Avalos family became homeowners. Luis was also instrumental in helping David be part of a group selected for police training at the San Diego Police Academy a few years back.

"We need to have targets. Any clues or information we get will be analyzed. Then a decision will be made based on the evidence. OK?"

"Fine," Javier agreed. Then offered, "If new information comes along, we share it with few people; the less the better." If the federal police got wind somebody was sniffing around, asking questions about a case officially closed, serious repercussions would follow.

"Last," David said, "We need to be patient. Rosarito has only a handful of bars where people gather to brag about their dealings. Somebody with one beer too many is bound to show off and give us a clue. Something we can grab and go after."

The first clue came almost a year after the killings at the Punta Bandera Beach. Don Ramon called and asked them to come right away. "There is a guy here sitting with a group, drinking, saying interesting things."

When Javier and David arrived at *La Tortuga* restaurant they sat at a table near the large window and ordered a couple of beers. Don Ramon came to their table and discreetly pointed to a person sitting at a corner table with four other men.

"The scruffy looking guy came here last week. He bragged about doing work for some bad-ass guys from Tijuana. I thought it was beer talk. Everybody wants to be a *narco* nowadays. Today he told the guy sitting next to him life's good; he's helping an American and three Mexicans move drugs across the border. He also said he was resentful he got short-changed by some *putos gringos* a year ago, doing a job here in Rosarito, at Punta Bandera Beach."

Javier and David stared at the guy.

"Can you find out who he is?" David asked.

"I'll ask around," Don Ramon replied, as he walked away from the table.

A couple of weeks later Don Ramon had information. The guy's name was Manuel Aguilar and he commuted from Rosarito to Tijuana on weekends. As far as anybody knew, Manuel was just another wannabe *narco* tough guy. He lived in the south part of Rosarito and spent Friday and Saturday nights at *La Parrilla* Restaurant in the Mesa de Otay, a few blocks south of the Otay Mesa Border checkpoint in Tijuana.

One Saturday night Manuel was followed to Mesa de Otay. Manuel met three other Mexicans at a restaurant near the border check point, in front of a local park. The family restaurant was the perfect location to spy on people. The front section of the restaurant had glass, allowing the public a glance at the customers inside. David and Javier sat on one of the park benches across the street, lost among the traffic and the people moving about along the street.

It was easy to assess Manuel's role within the group. When all the members got together at the family restaurant, Manuel's participation was minimal. During the group's conversations he nodded and uttered yes and no answers. At times he was asked to go outside and keep an eye on things. The meetings didn't go past 10:00 p.m. on Fridays or Saturdays.

It was a different story on Sunday nights in Rosarito. Manuel talked as if he was the patriarch of a mafia family. The guy appeared useless, but when he kept mentioning the incident at Punta Bandera Beach, Javier and David knew he had been involved, or at least knew something about Luis and Ramiro's deaths.

It became routine to take dinner and a couple of newspapers and just sit at one of the park benches and observe Manuel and the rest of the group eat and drink at the restaurant in the Mesa de Otay area. In order to break the monotony, they gave Manuel a name: Don Corleone.

Thirteen

As time went by, Javier and David became frustrated and scared. They had one individual and nothing else. If by coincidence, Don Corleone produced a name or a place, then what? Do they go to the police?

Even with solid evidence, there was a strong possibility the police might not be interested in solving the Punta Bandera Beach killings. If a police officer or politician with strong connections to the federal government was involved, it was a death warrant for both families.

During one of the weekend meetings an American walked in and joined the group. Before the American sat at the table, Don Corleone and another guy were asked to leave. Don Corleone was not pleased. Even from a distance the anger was painted on his face. Don Corleone and the other guy waited outside the restaurant.

"The Don is pissed," Javier said.

"Who is the American?" David wondered.

Inside the restaurant the meeting lasted a few minutes. The American talked and the other two men listened and nodded in agreement. But something was off: Javier and David had expected an imposing individual with an attitude about himself, flashing extreme wealth. There was nothing distinguishing about the American. He had brown hair, average height and weight and wore simple street clothes and an Adidas warm-up jacket. Was this the *gringo* Don Corleone was complaining about?

"An American comes in for a short meeting and the Don gets kicked out: planning a drug deal?" David wondered.

"Maybe," Javier answered.

The American returned six weeks later. This time Don Corleone stayed for the meeting. It was a break in the investigation. Don Corleone was privy to the information being tossed around at the meetings by the Mexicans and the American.

The investigation reached a crossroads. Sitting at a park bench and observing people talk inside a restaurant lost its value. Don Corleone had some information and there was no choice but to take it away from him.

There was a problem. Once the information

was taken from Don Corleone, they couldn't let him walk away. They had to kill him. There was no other choice. But can police officers searching for justice take a man's life with freedom from punishment? Can a family man kill a person in cold blood and then go home to hug and kiss his wife and kids without remorse?

After nights of unrest David came to a conclusion. His logic derived from guilt and fairness. After years of hardship due to the Apartheid form of government, the South African people were able to reconcile, to forgive and move on with their lives. Following the 1994 Rwanda genocide, the Tutsi people were able to reconcile with their killers, the Hutus. In life we pay for our sins. If you are a Christian you repent and ask for forgiveness, and if it's a grievous offence, you pay it in hell. If you don't have a religion you look within yourself to make wrong things right.

The killers of Luis and Ramiro are not going to a San Diego criminal court because the information collected is coming from people south of the border. The American legal system always protects their own. The Baja California state and federal legal systems, on the other hand, didn't have the need or desire to open an investigation aimed at scrutinizing the way their own particular bureaus handle their criminal investigations. It would be political suicide for many local, state, and federal police officials.

David sensed there was a strong possibility other families had lost a loved one during a drug transaction along the beaches of Tijuana, Rosarito and Ensenada over the last five years. They had to find and stop the people responsible for the deaths of Luis and Ramiro; otherwise many more families would suffer the same pain and degradation they had endured. They had to view Don Corleone as collateral damage.

Fourteen

Life was moving in the right direction. Don Corleone was feeling good about his future. A stroke of luck came his way in the form of a guy named Mario. After months of nurturing a secret relationship with Mario, it finally paid off. Mario shared the names of people in charge of moving cocaine across the Mesa de Otay-Otay Mesa Border checkpoint. It was three Americans and four Mexicans. The guy in charge was a DEA agent but Mario was doing business on the side with a younger American, a Border Patrol agent. Mario asked Don Corleone to join his small group.

Don Corleone was feeling elated as he walked out of *La Tortuga* restaurant and got into his vehicle. He pulled out of the parking lot and made a right turn, heading south on Avenida Juarez. Unnoticed, a light blue car was following him, keeping a safe distance between cars.

Avenida Juarez was busy with people, mostly tourists walking along the avenue enjoying the cool air of the night. Many people walked from bar to bar, listening to music and dancing along the sidewalk. The neon lights lit up the avenue like a carnival.

Don Corleone drove south along the avenue absorbing the sights and sounds without a care in the world. As he passed the Rosarito Beach Resort Hotel, the unofficial end of the tourist strip, the car slowed down. Poor street lighting and uneven pavement made driving precarious. As the neon lights from the avenue faded, Don Corleone saw a red light flashing in his rear-view mirror. He waited until he found a wide space, away from traffic, before pulling over. Once he parked the car on the side of the road, he left the lights on and waited for the police officers to come and talk to him. It was nothing two twenty-dollar bills couldn't handle.

Don Corleone didn't bother pulling out his driving license or car registration. Looking at the rear-view mirror, he was surprised when two police officers got out of the car, weapons drawn. One came to his side and asked him to step outside. After he got out the other police officer guided him by the shoulder to the front of the car, away from traffic. The police officers did not exchange words. Like in

Hollywood movies, he was asked to spread his legs and place his open palms on top of the hood of the car. Things were moving in the wrong direction; the hairs on his neck stood up and a chill ran up his spine.

"Hey, what the hell are you doing?"

No response.

"Motherfuckers, I'm talking to you!"

Silence.

Fear plastered the skin; he felt goose bumps forming on his arms. He was being patted down, and he did not know why. Quickly, one of the police officers placed a handgun to his right temple while the other officer hand cuffed him.

"Goddamn it! Stop this shit!" Don Corleone protested. "What the hell did I do?" He yelled.

One of the officers walked him to the patrol car, opened the rear door and threw him on the floor. After closing and securing the car's back door, the officer opened the driver's side door and got in. The other officer walked to Don Corleone's car to turn off the lights. With slow steps the officer returned, opened the back door and sat on the back seat with his feet on top of Don Corleone. As the car drove away Don Corleone could feel the small bumps on the road hit his chest and hear the car tires rolling on top of the loose gravel.

There was no traffic.

The patrol car drove south and four miles later turned east, across Interstate 1, towards the town's landfill. They drove for another three miles. The lights of the downtown area were no longer visible when the car stopped near a low bank. The car headlights stayed on, illuminating some low bushes and a group of large boulders. He was taken out of the car and made to sit on one of the boulders.

Don Corleone was disoriented and terrified.

While one of the police officers held a gun to the back of his head, the other opened the trunk and removed items from a plastic bag. The police officer came back with two rolls of duct tape. Without speaking he quickly started to tape Don Corleone's arms to his body. He then removed his shoes and socks and taped his legs together above his knees. A piece of tape was placed across his mouth. The police officer walked back to the car, carrying the rolls of duct tape with him.

Don Corleone was beyond being terrified; he knew his life was on the line. He had something they wanted or he did something to them. He did not recognize the two police officers. Who the hell were they, and what did they want?

Seconds later the police officer returned from the car, and stood in front of him. He was holding a piece of duct tape in his right hand; his left hand was behind his back. The officer looked straight into his eyes and held the stare for a couple of seconds. Don Corleone got the message: something bad was going to happen to him. When the duct tape was placed to cover his eyes, he started to sweat and a wave of panic engulfed him.

Don Corleone felt his feet being placed flatly on top of a boulder. Felt the sandy, loose soil of the boulder rubbing against the bottom of his feet.

Then silence.

Nothing occurred for the next few seconds. Then a shockwave hit his brain. The pain started in the small toes of his right leg and then traveled to his brain and back again. The pain was so intense his foot became numb. The neurons in his brain were firing in all directions and at twice the speed of light. Then another shock wave, this time from the large toes. A solid and heavy object was pounding on his toes, smashing the flesh and bones against the boulder. Mucus flew out of his nostrils. Breathing became laborious. He tried to yell at the top of his lungs but the duct tape across his mouth muffled his screams. He knew he was crying but the duct tape was holding back the tears. His right foot was numb and his brain was pounding. Slowly the duct tape was removed from his eyes. His vision was blurry from the tears and the pain. He wanted to hold his foot, to massage his toes, but couldn't. The foot felt ten times its normal size and the pain—it was impossible to describe.

Holding a sledge hammer, the police officer stood in front of him.

"Your toes are fractured; they are useless. If you have some savings from your business dealing with the American, you can go to San Diego and get medical attention. A decent doctor will fix you, not completely, but good enough for you to walk with a limp. If you don't have any money, you are out of luck; we don't have doctors here trained well enough to repair your toes. Your foot will be useless."

There was a pause.

"Listen to me carefully. I am going to ask you a few questions, and all I want from you is to give us the answers. Don't play games; you don't have anything to bargain with. If you don't answer correctly I will finish the toes of your right foot, work on your knee and then I will do the same with the left leg. If I have to, I will also work on your arms. By the time they find you, no doctor will be able to fix you. Do you understand?"

The image painted by the police officer was enough to convince Don Corleone to cooperate.

Death was not an option right now, not when things were going so well for him.

The police officer sat on a boulder and placed the sledge hammer in front of Don Corleone. From the pocket of his jacket the officer produced a small tape recorder.

"Please answer the questions completely, do not leave anything out. Talk slow and clear to the tape recorder. Do you understand?"

Don Corleone nodded in agreement.

It was a painful and deserving ending for Don Corleone. He died of massive injuries and was buried in a deep grave far away from town. Nobody was going to find him.

On the way home Javier and David were silent. They were mentally exhausted. They had the information they needed, and what they wanted now was to go home and to sleep for a long time.

Fifteen

The following night David and Javier sat alone at *La Tortuga* Restaurant after it closed for business. Don Ramon placed the food on the table and walked back to the kitchen. He knew they had information and in due time they would share it with him.

With paper and pencils in front of them they played the tape of the confession.

Shaking from a mixture of pain and fear Don Corleone described how every six to eight weeks, two Americans and a group of Mexicans met at different spots along the north section of Rosarito Beach, to make drug transactions. The Americans came in cars and the helpers in dark-colored vans. The vehicles parked at the edge of the beach and then waited for small boats to bring the drugs to shore.

There was a pause. A bag of ice was placed on top of the right foot of Don Corleone. Whiskey from a bottle was poured into a plastic cup. David put the plastic cup to the lips of Don Corleone. He eagerly took two long gulps. After gaining some composure Don Corleone continued.

Everything was done quickly and quietly. Don Corleone's job varied according to the situation; from securing the beach, to helping place the drugs inside the vans. There were two Americans in charge of the operation, but every now and then another American would show up. He never participated. He was different: he dressed better, and he didn't give out orders. The first two Americans were government officers; they said that to the group at their first meeting, but the fancy dresser didn't say what he did for a living. The name of the oldest was Tom; Sam was the younger officer, and Stewart was the well-dressed guy.

There was another pause. This time Don Corleone took one long swallow of whiskey and two percocet tablets.

During a drug transaction Don Corleone and the rest of the group came upon Luis and Ramiro and they didn't know what to do. They had two people, two witnesses. First they hit them with their fists and later they used the butts of their assault rifles. Don Corleone believed Ramiro and Luis when they said they were local police officers, and so did the other Mexicans in the group. They had met Rosarito police officers before and they knew what police badges look like. But the Americans didn't care, especially Tom. He told the group he was afraid of everybody being identified and caught by the Rosarito Police. The Mexicans told Tom the local police guys were harmless, who could they tell? When Tom said to kill them, everyone was shocked, but they had to follow orders. It was Stewart's idea to leave cocaine in one of the tents to confuse the Rosarito Police.

La Parrilla Restaurant was an ideal place for the group to meet; it was close to the border checkpoint and most of the group lived in Tijuana. Don Corleone and another guy from the group lived in Rosarito. At the meetings only a select few were invited. Don Corleone was not one of them. He didn't hide his resentment at not being invited to the inner circle. He had participated at different levels of the operation and had been part of two homicides. He had earned the right to be there. At the meetings Tom provided only the essential information based on its level of importance. Don Corleone was delegated to do the dirty work and got paid between three to five thousand dollars, which he considered bullshit.

They stop one more time to get a blanket for Don Corleone. The temperature had dropped and he had started to shiver. They gave him another drink. The confession continued.

The Don was happy because his luck was beginning to change. A guy named Mario invited him to separate meetings held by Sam. They did small transactions in the same area, just north of Rosarito Beach. He was happy because he was able to make another ten thousand dollars and felt he was on track to move up the ladder and make a lot more money. Looking at both officers he said he was sorry if somebody they knew got hurt. If they wanted to join the group, he could put in a good word for them.

Almost three hours later the whirling sound coming from the tape recorder indicated the audio tape had come to the end. David grabbed the tape recorder and pressed the stop button. The spinning noise stopped with the sound of the click.

The confession painted an ugly picture of greed and abuse of power.

"Shit. . . I'm trying, but I don't understand. Don Corleone and the rest of the group beat the shit out of Luis and Ramiro because they were at the wrong place?" David asked, and then added, "And

Tom said to kill them. And the group followed the orders?"

Rubbing the pencil with his thumb and forefinger Javier said, "Nobody cared they were local police officers and had families. Both were people. Luis and Ramiro were discarded like two cigarette butts thrown out of a speeding car window without a drop of remorse, or fear of retribution."

Sixteen

The disappearance of Don Corleone from local bars in Rosarito didn't attract much attention. Life went on, and few people asked questions about his whereabouts. Others assumed he was away somewhere in Tijuana looking for an opportunity to make a quick dollar.

Javier and David visited some of the popular bars and restaurants along Avenida Juarez and discretely asked waiters and waitresses if anybody had inquired, or raised concerns about Don Corleone's whereabouts.

Nobody did.

They decided to drive to the Mesa de Otay restaurant in Tijuana and observe a meeting without Don Corleone being present. To protect themselves David invited a female friend of his from Tijuana. It was a woman he knew and trusted since his teen-age years. David only provided general information about the need to sit in front of a restaurant for a few hours, and she, in return, was clever enough not to ask for details.

The meeting at the local restaurant was a surprise. Tom, the tall gray-haired American made an appearance. The meeting was different. Tom talked at length, pausing only to take long swallows from a Dos Equis beer, while the group sat, listened and nodded in agreement. The group did not seem to notice the absence of Don Corleone.

Across the street from the restaurant, lost among groups of people walking in different directions, David and his female friend sat on a concrete bench. David played with the woman's blouse and hair, but every now and then he managed to take a few glances toward the restaurant.

When the meeting ended, Tom walked out of the restaurant, almost bumping into a young mother leading her child by the hand. David waited a few seconds before getting up and slowly walking in the same direction along the sidewalk. Tom walked along the street with his hands inside the pockets of his dark windbreaker. He moved easily with the flow of pedestrians. Tom strolled past the small shops for about a block, and then stopped in front of a dark Honda parked next to a concrete street light post. Using the light post as protection, he stood behind it. Motionless, he waited a few seconds before looking back, scanning the street for people, cars or anything else that indicated he had been followed. Leaning back against the concrete light post he removed the car keys from the front pocket of his jeans and walked towards the trunk of the Honda. Using the clicker he disarmed the car's alarm. When the trunk was opened, he looked behind him and swiftly removed the gun from the back of his waist and placed it under a mat, next to the spare tire. With a quick slam he closed the trunk of the car, and with long steps walked to the driver's side of the car and without hesitation got in. After locking the door he inserted the key into the ignition and quickly started the car's engine. Waiting only a few seconds for the traffic to clear, he aggressively pulled into the street and drove away. About a hundred feet away, right in the middle of the narrow intersection, he made a sharp u-turn, forcing the vehicles moving in both directions to slam on their brakes. The screeching sounds coming from the tires sliding on the asphalt and cars honking, forced pedestrians to look at the Honda as it peeled away along the street. Tom appeared unfazed by the commotion as he pressed on the gas pedal. As the Honda moved along the narrow street, David and his female friend stopped and kissed; David held the woman's face with his hands, blocking his face from the Honda. David took a quick look at the license plates and made a mental note: This man is good! He created a traffic jam to get away and to ensure he was not followed.

When the Honda reached the corner, it made a left turn into the one-way street leading to the Otay Mesa Border checkpoint.

When the Honda disappeared from sight, David looked at his female companion with complete attention. Leaning forward David held her face with his hands again, and kissed her softly. He whispered something to her, which made her smile. As he embraced her again, she responded by wrapping her arms around his neck, allowing David to use his right hand to place dollar bills inside the woman's blouse.

Across the street, lost among pedestrians, Javier walked on the outside part of the sidewalk. He wore a dark blue corduroy jacket, and carried a folded newspaper in his right hand. As he passed by the concrete light post, he changed the newspaper to his left hand, and briefly stopped to look at his wrist watch. It was a signal; it meant nobody had followed them. Seconds later he was lost among the crowd.

David guided his female friend along the street. As they approached an alley, David squeezed the woman's hand and gently let it go. He walked into the alley and disappeared in the shadows. The woman continued to walk without missing a beat. At the corner of the street she paused briefly for the traffic light to turn green. She didn't look in any direction and continued to walk for a couple of more blocks before she signaled for a taxi.

Seventeen

After five years of conversations with friends and strangers, searching for evidence, and surveillance, Javier and David knew they had come to a dead end. Going after Americans in San Diego without help from somebody with law enforcement experience was a monumental task.

Don Ramon decided it was time to get involved. He kept track of the investigation and crossing the border was extremely dangerous. If David or Javier got caught in San Diego, family members paid the consequences. He phoned Javier and David and invited them to an early breakfast.

When both arrived at the restaurant the next day, Don Ramon was seated at a table drinking his coffee. Both pulled out a chair and sat down. Don Ramon raised his hand and signaled one of the waiters to bring two more cups of coffee. A young worker brought the cups of coffee, said hello to David and Javier and went back to the kitchen.

While Don Ramon talked about the weather and the local economy, Javier and David mixed their coffees.

When they were ready, Don Ramon was the first to speak.

"I knew Don Florentino for many years; we grew up together. We first met in elementary school and together we grew older; we got married and then our kids got married and started their own families. Florentino and I started this restaurant. It was my idea. Sixty percent of the financial support came from him and his family and the rest from mine. But I invested more than money; I brought the love for food and the devotion of having people congregate in one special place and break bread. To me a restaurant is more then just a place to eat; it's a sanctuary. This restaurant has been part of our lives for many years and it has been witness to countless family celebrations."

He paused to take a sip of coffee. Pointing to David and then to Javier he continued, "I have known both of you since you were children, I have always considered you part of my family. That is why the senseless deaths of Luis and Ramiro were difficult to accept, and that was the reason I got involved. For five years I've watched you guys conduct your investigation and I've been respectful; I haven't asked questions but I've made my own analysis and came to my own conclusions. It's now time for us to talk about what you've done and what needs to be completed for one important reason: protection. If something happens to both of you, I need to know who, and what, we are going up against."

Don Ramon moved the cups to the side of the table, clearing a spot in the center. "Place your papers here and tell me all you know."

Using their notes from the tape recordings Javier explained in detail everything they had discovered about the torture and killings of Luis and Ramiro. The papers and notes were arranged in a timeline form; Don Corleone: the meetings at *La Parrilla* Restaurant; the pictures of the participants and license plates; the tape recording of Don Corleone; his disappearance; and other details. Javier concluded, "We don't have anybody else to chase or interrogate. The next move is crossing the border and going after the three Americans, but we have no resources or information. We don't know how to make the next move. We need help."

"Maybe I can be of use." Don Ramon removed a piece of paper from his shirt pocket and placed it on the table. It was a business card.

"Javier, on your mother's side you have a relative who works with the San Diego Police

Department. His name is Manny Mendez. Your grandmother and his grandmother were sisters. But the families drifted apart when the Mendez family moved to National City. When your parents died they came to the funeral and visited you twice before you came to Rosarito to live with Don Florentino. Beatriz, Manny's mother, came to see you twice when you moved here. Later they kept their distance because all your family members agreed you needed time to adjust to your new family. Mendez's constantly asked about you. They contributed money to your trust fund. They came to Luis and Ramiro's funerals but they didn't ask questions because they felt uncomfortable. Since they had stayed away for so long they didn't know what to say or ask. The Mendez family still lives in National City and like I said, your cousin Manny works with the San Diego Police Department, in the homicide division."

When Don Ramon got up from the table to get more coffee, Javier turned to David and said, "Shit! Do you believe this?"

Don Ramon came back with a large pot of coffee, placed it on the table and sat down. "The Mendez family is coming next Saturday, so let's get organized so we can provide Manny with the proper information."

Javier looked at David and then at Don Ramon. "Don Ramon, I don't know how to say this. We are not going to arrest the Americans, and then turn them over to the police. We are not sure what we are going to do with them."

"I understand," Don Ramon responded. "I will not compromise your investigation; although I have a pretty good feeling Manny will help regardless of the situation. I will keep your notes and organize the information. First, let's eat breakfast and afterward you can go home to tell your families to get ready for the family reunion this coming Saturday."

At home Javier told his wife and daughter about his new-found family members, particularly his cousin Manny, and the family reunion. He gave details about the Mendez family, but kept the contents of the meeting with David and Don Ramon in general terms. Angelica was happy for him and for the family; it meant all of them had more people to visit and create community with. She was disappointed at not being able to learn details of the meeting. A full explanation was out of the question, but she felt a sense of ineptitude not knowing in what direction the investigation was moving and how to protect her family.

At the beginning, the family reunion at the restaurant lacked a family ambiance; although related by blood there had not been enough encounters throughout the years for Javier and Manny and the rest of their families to create a bond. Don Ramon, however, had prepared for this occasion. The families were asked to bring family pictures, especially those which connected Manny, Luis, Ramiro, David and Javier.

After a breakfast of orange juice, eggs, bacon, coffee, tea and grapefruit juice, Don Ramon asked a couple of workers to clear the two largest tables and place them together. When the dishes and food items were removed from the tables, Don Ramon invited everyone to sit around the tables and to take out their family photographs. With care, thick photo albums were placed on the tables, along with single photos of different sizes. The photos were the catalyst: smiling, family members pointed to the photos recalling a time, or a place, and events from years gone by. Within a few minutes the gathering acquired a festive mood.

Beatriz Mendez got up from her seat and moved towards Javier. A white envelope was in her left hand. She pulled up a chair and sat next to him. She had long gray hair in a pony tail and a beautiful smile. The envelope was placed on the table. With her delicate fingers, she removed a black and white photograph. The photo showed two young girls, arms around each other, smiling, full of youth.

"Your mother and I were more than just cousins, we were best friends," her voice came out with emotion. "We were young, idealistic, and had high hopes. Unfortunately my family moved to National City, and it became difficult for us to stay in touch. We did our best to write to each other but it was not the same." Tears started to roll down her face.

Javier stared at the photograph on the table and didn't reply; there was nothing to say. He took the picture from her hand and carefully analyzed it. Beatriz and his mother had been two good-looking young women in their youth.

"You can have the picture; it is my gift to you. I want you to remember your mother when she was full of life and hope." She slowly got up from her chair, moved to Javier and holding his face with her hands she said, "If your mother was here she would be proud of you. I promise you, this time it is going to be different. Starting today, all of us are going to stay in touch and form a family bond. I understand you have a meeting soon, so I will let you get ready." She kissed him on the forehead and then walked away.

Javier watched Beatriz walk away and then glanced at the rest of the crowd congregated around the tables, talking and laughing. He was not alone in this world; he had found more family members, and with them, strong moral support.

As the families enjoyed ice cream, Don Ramon, Javier, David and Manny walked downstairs to the parking lot. All of them got into Don Ramon's SUV, pulled out of the parking lot and drove south to the Rosarito Beach Hotel. Instead of sitting at one of the benches by the small shops, they went for a walk along the beach.

Due to the legal and moral issues involved with the investigation, Don Ramon asked Manny the following questions: do you want to learn only the details related to the Americans and the killings of Luis and Ramiro, or do you want to learn the entire investigation, including the possibility of not arresting the Americans after you find them?

Manny wanted to know everything.

Don Ramon laid out the facts in as much detail as possible, explaining what they had discovered in the last five years. Javier and David added details as the conversation went along. Manny asked questions at different intervals, sometimes asking the same question twice. After the conversation died down, they walked back to the car in silence.

Standing next to the SUV, Manny looked at Javier and said, "I am sorry about Luis and Ramiro, Javier. We all know what they meant to you and to your family." Turning to David he added, "David, you placed your life on hold to help Javier in this crusade. I find that incredible."

Javier and David only smiled. The last five years had been a physical and emotional roller coaster, impossible to describe.

"I am impressed with the investigation; you had nothing to guide you but your own instincts and common sense. And here we are, with enough information to arrest and possibly prosecute those agents in an American court. I want you to know it is sickening to find out federal people are responsible for the deaths of Luis and Ramiro. But it doesn't matter; I will get the information you need to find the agents." Manny approached Javier and hugged him for a few seconds. Then he turned and hugged David.

They drove back to the restaurant and re-joined their families. The gathering lasted into the late afternoon. At the end of the festivities the members promised to stay in touch and to have a family reunion once a year. Javier and David were the last to leave the restaurant. Now the impetus of the investigation depended on Manny. Before leaving the restaurant he reminded everyone that finding the names and addresses of the agents was a slow process requiring time and patience.

After five years of investigating all the possible leads, Don Ramon, Javier and David were ready for a well-deserved rest.

Eighteen

Encinitas, California
Monday December 21, 2009

Tom Peterson returned from his four-mile morning walk along South Coast Highway. He stopped at the local Starbucks to buy a medium Café Americano, and now he was heading back to his house on Cornish Drive. After his visit with Chino and his girlfriend yesterday, his intuition told him Chino lied. The guy had information, but the question was, how much?

There was no choice but to go back later in the afternoon and have another chat with him and his girlfriend. Hurting people was not fun, but it was a necessary evil.

Inside his house he went to the kitchen and put down the coffee cup by the sink. He washed his hands and then walked to his bedroom. The small digital clock by the nightstand displayed the time; it was 7:29 a.m. The woman asleep on the bed stirred. She lay on her stomach, her blond hair covering the left part of her face. He sat on the edge of the bed and reached for his cell phone. He dialed the numbers and then placed the phone to his right ear. The phone started to ring on the other end. After a few rings somebody answered.

"Yes?"

"Are you coming to the office today?" Tom used a calm voice.

"Yes," replied the voice on the other end.

"Please stop by my office. I have some papers that need your signature."

"Fine. What time?"

"At one p.m. Is that OK?"

"Yes." And the line went dead.

Tom closed the lid to the phone and placed it back on the stand. The son of a bitch sounds upset. "Oh, well," he said to himself.

Nineteen

Fallbrook, California
Monday December 21, 2009

Samuel Davis was sitting at the kitchen table having a cup of coffee and reading the morning newspaper when the phone rang. He picked it up on the third ring.

"Hello."

"This is a courtesy call. We are closing the store for inventory today. Please pick up your merchandise as soon as possible. We'll call you again when we re-open."

"Fine, I'll do it right away," Samuel answered. Is Tom closing the business for the rest of the year? Right now, during the Christmas season? Sam was confused.

Sam was still thinking about the phone call, and holding the phone in his right hand, when his wife Carol walked into the kitchen.

"Is everything OK?" She asked, with a concerned look.

"Yeah, I just forgot to sign some papers," Sam replied, avoiding her gaze, placing the phone back in the receiver. He grabbed the car keys from the kitchen counter and started to walk towards the front door.

"Are you leaving? Are you going to work? It's your day off! " Carol asked, irritated. She stood in the kitchen, arms akimbo, upset at her husband for walking away without an explanation. "You told the kids we were going shopping and then later to the movies."

Sam turned around and waiving the keys said, "I'm just going to the station to sign some forms and then I'll come right back. I'll be gone for a few minutes." He opened the door and walked out, not waiting for a reply.

Sam drove to Main Street Nursery, located near Interstate15, about five miles from his home. It was the usual meeting place. Sam parked his car facing the freeway. With long steps he walked past the cashier's stand, past the rose bushes, ficus trees, and into the large shaded area where they kept all the indoor plants and trees. He stood there, pretending to be another customer, mingling with the rest of the people. Somehow he knew Tom would find him.

It didn't take long.

In a simple tone somebody behind him said, "Pretty azaleas, don't you think?"

Sam turned and looked towards the person talking but didn't answer. He hated all this preamble nonsense. Today he had no patience for any bullshit; all he wanted was to get this meeting over with, and then go home. Sam turned and looked in different directions to see if anybody was watching them.

"What's the matter, don't you like azaleas?"

"Let's cut the bullshit, what's going on?" Sam asked without looking at Tom.

Smiling Tom said, "Fine, I'll get to the point. We have a fucking problem. I was told by somebody I trust, your friend Mario kept a log, a list of places, names and phone numbers, and gave them to a guy named Chino, his girlfriend, and maybe to other people I don't know. If the information is floating around, we are fucked."

Tom waited for Sam's reaction.

"Are you sure?" Sam's voice got edgy. He knew it was his responsibility to call people and let them know when to come across the Temecula and Otay Mesa checkpoints. Tom was implying he had been sloppy, that it was his fault.

Tom picked up a one-gallon container plant,

pretending to look at the price. "Yes, I am sure. We need to get the information back from Chino tonight, one way or another."

"Bullshit. If the information is out, it is not my fault; I was careful—very careful," Sam interrupted, taking a defensive position.

Tom noticed the edginess in Sam's voice. Nobody was accusing him, yet he was placing the blame on somebody else. He's not concerned about the group, he thought, only in protecting himself.

Shit, this was not a good sign.

Tom decided not to press Sam. Instead he smiled and said, "Nobody's accusing you, Sam. Please relax."

Tom walked a few steps and picked up another one-gallon container. "I'm meeting with Stewart later today. In the meantime, everything stops until further notice. We need to visit Chino tonight; I will call you and let you know the time. Your money is in your car. I'll be in touch." Tom moved the container near his face; he wanted to smell the emerging buds of the gardenia he was holding. Smiling, he said, "I think I'll buy this one." He started to walk towards the cashier's stand.

Sam waited a couple of minutes before walking out of the nursery. When he got into his car he saw the familiar bulky manila envelope on the floor on the passenger side. There were forty thousand dollars in one-hundred-dollar bills inside the manila envelope, his percentage for this month.

Sam was disappointed with the amount.

Many promises had been made to his wife and kids about taking a vacation and buying many things for the house and for themselves. Fuck!

The money inside the envelope was not enough to pay for the things he had promised his wife and family. Sam pulled his car out of the parking lot, making mental calculations.

Twenty

Downtown, San Diego
Monday December 21, 2009

Tom Peterson pulled into the parking lot and stopped at the booth to collect his parking stub from the parking lot attendant. The parking lot was located right across the street from the Santa Fe Railroad Depot in downtown San Diego. He got out of the vehicle, locked the car, put on his sunglasses, and started walking west on Broadway Street. At the corner of Kettner and Broadway he stopped and waited for the traffic light to change. When the traffic light turned green, as a precaution, he waited for a mom with a stroller and a group of young people to go ahead of him. As he crossed the street he glanced back to the parking lot, and then north, to where the *Star of India* ship was docked. There was a line of people waiting to board the large ship. At a slow pace he started to mingle with the crowd. He continued to walk past Pacific Street and Harbor

Drive carefully looking around making sure he was not being followed. He stopped at the San Diego Cruise Ship Terminal booth and bought a round trip ticket for the San Diego to Coronado Ferry. At the small gate he gave one of his tickets to the young attendant. Once he was on board the ferry he quickly walked along the metal benches, and then up the few steps leading to the top of the ferry. From the top he had a clear view of the back of the ferry and its passengers.

Tom saw Stewart come on board, staying in the shaded area, away from the sunlight, right below the pilot's cabin. Stewart had always been concerned with skin cancer.

He's probably reading the Wall Street Journal, always pretending to be somebody else, that pompous son of a bitch, Tom said to himself.

The ferry left the Broadway Pier at twelve-thirty for its fifteen-minute ride to Coronado Island. Having a clear view of the upper deck, Tom tried to guess the identities of the other passengers. Young couples sat close together holding hands, pointing to the water and to the Coronado Bridge a few miles away.

Students, said Tom to himself.

Families with young children, some in strollers, sat looking at maps. Boring tourists, he guessed.

Two Mexicans wearing baseball caps sat next to each other holding Mexican newspapers and leather working gloves. Gardeners, illegal aliens, he guessed, again.

The rest of the passengers were uninteresting.

At the landing, Tom was one of the first to step onto the pier. At a fast pace he followed the concrete sidewalk leading to the local shops. Instead of walking into one of the shops, he kept walking, and a short distance later, he found a concrete bench and sat down. From his position he had a clear view of the landing and the passengers disembarking. Tom marveled at the irony of the situation. He was a federal agent sure of himself, with military experience and trained to kill. Stewart was a banker, pampered from birth, a fraud. He led a life of luxury at the expense of his investors. Yet, both needed each other.

Stewart came to shore with his usual floppy hat protecting his blond hair and sensitive skin. A newspaper tucked inside his arm. With calculated steps he walked along the pathway, looking at the passengers and the people congregated at the small plaza in the middle of the shops. He turned and fixed his eyes on Tom as he passed the shops. Tom turned his head to look at the ocean and at the Embarcadero Marina Park. Without talking or acknowledging Tom, Stewart sat on the concrete bench, letting out a sigh.

"What seems to be the problem?" Stewart asked, with a tone that implied more than just annoyance.

Tom didn't reply. Still facing the ocean Tom took a drink from his water bottle.

Stewart sat at the edge of the concrete bench, a clear sign of irritation. He had been forced to spend part of his day playing a cloak-and-dagger bullshit game he detested, instead of a morning round of golf at The Torrey Pines Country Club.

Tom remained still. He took another sip of water, stalling. He was being insulted by a lowlife piece of shit, but to show annoyance would be an admittance Stewart had gotten under his skin, had broken his discipline. And that could never happen, not with this piece of shit.

"I know for a fact that our dear friend Sam has been dealing, doing business on the side." Tom was choosing his words carefully. He knew Stewart and Samuel had a long and strong relationship.

"Sam has been making deals on the side for the last seven months or maybe longer. He travels across the border on a regular basis, the last time two weeks ago. I know because he meets with his group at *La Parrilla* Restaurant in Mesa de Otay, in

Tijuana. Sam is not fucking smart, is he?" The last words came out with venom. It implied: if Sam is not smart, and he's your best friend, then that also makes you a Goddamn fool.

Stewart was not lured. He remained silent.

Tom had another sip of water and said, "He also used Mario on this side of the border. Mario went along because Sam promised him all sorts of things." Tom paused to allow his words to sink in; he wanted to make sure Stewart knew they had a serious problem.

"But Mario wasn't stupid," Tom continued. "He kept a log of the dates in which he crossed the Otay Mesa-Mesa de Otay and Temecula check points. There is also a list of phone numbers for different agents, including Sam's, yours and mine. Sam got sloppy and compromised us. This is a serious problem and I take responsibility for not keeping track of everybody. Until everything is sorted out, we are not doing any more dealings."

Stewart's shoulders sagged. Tom didn't have to look at his face to know what Stewart was thinking. Stewart's stomach was turning in many directions. His face was pale.

"When Mario died, I thought the situation was under control. But we didn't find notes or a driving log when we searched his room. People told us he became good friends with a guy named Chino and I believe this Chino somehow got a hold of the information." Tom paused for a few seconds and then turned; he wanted to see the expression on Stewart's face. But Stewart didn't react, instead kept looking straight across the bay, lost in concentration.

"I met with Sam this morning. Of course, he denied everything. It always comes to money, Stewart. Sam got fucking greedy. I checked and he's been spending money all over the place and pretty soon somebody is bound to get suspicious. Sam has become a liability."

Tom was enjoying the moment because he knew Stewart was being consumed by fear.

"I met Chino last Saturday night at *La Parrilla* Restaurant and then stopped by his place last night in Vista—" Tom stopped talking when he saw the two Mexican gardeners from the ferry walking towards them. He made eye contact with one of them, but the gardener didn't hold his stare. The Mexicans continued walking, talking in Spanish. Tom waited until the Mexicans were about a hundred feet away before turning in their direction, trying to catch one more glimpse. The Mexicans did not turn; they continued walking at the same slow pace.

Tom continued with the information, "As I

said, we had a conversation with Chino last night. A girl was with him. We got rough with both of them because I know he's guilty; he's hiding information. It's just too easy for him to show up out of nowhere and say he wants to join our group." Tom finished drinking his water. He placed his left leg over his right, and rested his right arm over the backrest portion of the concrete bench. Tom was showing off, letting Stewart know he was cool under pressure.

"Tom, I think it would be best if all of us just stop dealing with drugs, and just walk away from everything." The words came out slow and without emotion. Stewart just sat facing the ocean, hands on his lap, his back barely touching the back portion of the bench.

"I wish life was that easy, Stewart, but it isn't," Tom replied.

"I'm out Tom. I don't want to be part of this anymore. I'm old and I'm tired." Stewart was trying to muster all the energy he had. He was trying his best to show a good front but it wasn't working.

Tom nodded and said, "I'm sorry, Stewart, but we are compromised. Sam placed us in a serious predicament and we need to finish—"
Stewart interrupted, "Don't you get it? I don't give a shit anymore! I'll take my chances with the law. If it comes down to it, I'll get a lawyer and make a deal.

Maybe I can—"

Before Stewart could finish, Tom cut in. "You fucking piece of shit! Do you think this is a fucking game? I'm a DEA agent, Sam is a Border Patrol officer and you are a fucking banker! I grabbed over a quarter of a million dollars from the evidence room, and then used my contacts in Tijuana to buy cocaine the first time. We have smuggled drugs across the border many times since then, and killed people, including two local cops from the other side of the border. I have risked my career and my life over and over. So what the fuck do you mean, 'I will make a deal!' Tom moved closer to Stewart and raised his index finger. "Not long ago you came to me. You spent millions of dollars from your customers betting on horses and living the high life. You were scared out of your mind. You knew you were going to jail, but I bailed you out. Remember?"

Stewart just sat there looking at Tom, lost in confusion.

Tom couldn't take it anymore. He raised his right hand and slapped Stewart hard across the face. Stewart lost his balance and fell off the bench. Slowly he picked himself up, but before he could sit on the bench again, Tom grabbed him by the shirt and shook him a couple of times.

"Listen to me, you fucking piece of shit! I'm

going back to pick up Sam later today and together we are going to find the missing names and phone numbers from Chino. Then I'll smooth things over with Sam about doing business on the side. Once that is accomplished, you can pull out, but not before. Do you fucking understand me?" Tom was breathing hard.

Stewart slightly nodded. The right side of his face was red; a welt was beginning to form. He was too scared and confused to contradict Tom.

"If you do anything stupid, I'll fucking kill you." With a shove Tom released Stewart. Stewart took short, awkward steps back, arms flailing, trying to regain his balance.

"Take a cab back to your car. I don't want you anywhere near me." Tom picked up the empty water bottle from the ground and started walking towards the pier.

Stewart stood there for a second watching Tom walk away. He straightened out his clothes and started walking towards the Burger King Restaurant on Orange Street. He wanted to rest and give Tom a chance to get to his car and drive away. The San Diego to Coronado ferry made a loop every fifteen minutes; he had plenty of time. He was serious when he said he wanted out of the business; he had had enough and he was not going to let anybody drag him around by a leash like a dog.

Yes, he had done something illegal, but he had repaid the money and the favors many times over. Yes, he had no stomach for smuggling drugs and hurting people but he had been there, lending moral support to Tom and Sam. But he was done opening illegal bank accounts, and more than anything, he was done being Tom's lackey.

Holding large plastic trash bags in each hand, and partially hidden behind a large carrotwood tree, David and Javier pretended to be city workers. They were replacing trash can liners along the concrete pathway. After Tom had taken the ferry back to San Diego and Stewart had disappeared from sight, Javier and David sat on a bench and tried to put all the pieces together.

David said, "Don't know what happened, but it must have been serious, because the banker got slapped hard on his face and didn't take the ferry back to San Diego."

Javier added, "The banker didn't fight back. Why? The DEA guy was mad about something; maybe he didn't get the response he wanted from the banker."

"What was the purpose of the meeting?" David asked.

"Bank accounts? The money they make has to

go someplace," Javier answered.

"Is that why the banker got hit?" David asked again.

"Maybe the banker refused to keep doing business with the DEA guy?" David wondered.

"Maybe the banker came up short with the drug money?" Javier said.

David and Javier didn't know the answers, but they knew something was falling apart; maybe the partnership was coming undone. They decided to drive to Tom's house in Encinitas. He will lead them to Sam. Later they could go after the banker.

Twenty-one

Encinitas, California
Monday December 21, 2009

Driving north along Highway 5, Tom was more than concerned. Things were beginning to unravel fast, first with Chino still holding information, and now Stewart, willing to arm himself with a lawyer, prepared to talk to the police. Was Stewart that dense? Did he actually believe drug trafficking and murder could be erased by turning state's evidence, and the San Diego Police and the federal court would just let him walk away? Knowing Stewart, the fucker would probably do it; but not in the near future, and not without a guarantee from the district attorney's office. He sighed. At the present time, however, Chino was the priority.

From home Tom called Sam and gave him an abbreviated version of the meeting with Stewart, omitting the slapping part and Stewart's desire to throw himself on the mercy of the federal court. Tom was careful with his words. Sam had become narrow minded, blinded by easy money and engulfed himself in his own sea of greediness. In that frame of mind Sam could fuck up and bring down the Border Patrol, U.S Customs and the police on them. Before ending the conversation Tom asked Sam to come to Vista with him to sit down with Chino and his girlfriend and get the information they needed from them.

Sam listened patiently without interruptions, but something was missing; his intuition told him something had gone wrong at the meeting. Tom had met with Stewart, and even though Tom hadn't said it, it didn't go well. Stewart was not invited to Vista. Sam feared Tom's plan was tilted against his best interests. Sam needed money to keep his wife and family happy. He had a bitch of a time coming up with an elaborate scheme to cover the real reason why the family couldn't take the vacation he promised them. Everything was moving along smoothly until Tom got paranoid about Mario keeping track of agents involved in their drug transactions. Sam was going to be patient and wait, but regardless of the outcome, he was making one business deal on his own to carry him through the

Christmas season. He was going to keep his wife and kids happy at any cost.

Twenty-two

Thomas Franklin Peterson was born in 1947 in the state of Arkansas, in a small town called Lubell, about two hundred miles northeast of Little Rock. It was a farming town with a population of about thirteen thousand people. His father owned a small grocery store and his mother stayed home to take care of the children. Thomas had no brothers and his two older sisters had married right after high school. In Lubell, life was simple. After high school almost everybody went into the farming business. A handful went to college, but the majority didn't venture outside of Lubell.

Thomas wanted more than farming or working in his father's grocery store. He knew there was a different world out there and wanted to see what lay beyond the horizon. The desire for adventure grew each time his uncle George came to visit. George Peterson was in the Navy and each time he came to visit he would talk for hours about the exotic places he had visited, like Japan, Indonesia and South Korea. He even saw other faraway countries with names difficult to remember and not easy to pronounce. Uncle George also talked about the big cities along the California coast, like San Francisco, Los Angeles and San Diego. Tom wanted to see this wonderful world and right after graduation from high school he joined the United States Marines.

Thomas joined the Marines in 1965, at a time when the United States, China and the Soviet Union were engaged in a costly rivalry which included military alliances, ideology, espionage, military, industrial and technological developments and the space race. In 1965 many soldiers were being sent to Viet Nam to fight a war never formally declared by Congress. South Vietnam, a poor defenseless country, was being attacked by the Communist government of the North. The United States had no choice but to help due to a treaty signed by President Kennedy. It was the domino theory: the Communists were determined to conquer the world, one country at a time. If not contained, Southeast Asia would fall to the Communists, then Europe and eventually the United States.

In the United States, many citizens were beginning to question the American involvement, especially as the number of casualties started to increase. What are we doing fighting a war so far away from home, many wanted to know. Thomas Peterson didn't care, he wanted to see the world, and if that meant going to a foreign land to fight a war that nobody understood or wanted, so be it.

The first destination after joining the Marines was San Diego. The thirteen weeks he spent at the United States Marine Corps Depot as part of the boot camp training were rigorous but enlightening. While most struggled with the marches and the long hours, Thomas enjoyed it because the physical pain was invigorating; it made him feel alive. Slowly he was beginning to understand how discipline played an important role in life.

After boot camp he was assigned to Camp Pendleton, north of Oceanside, California, for Infantry Training School. Camp Pendleton was the largest training camp for Marines in the Western part of the United States.

At Camp Pendleton, Marines trained with weapons, perfected their hand-to-hand combat skills, and learned ground-assault and battle formations. Marine recruits had to learn how to fight the enemy in different types of terrain, including the stifling heat of Viet Nam. They had to endure countless hours of Marine philosophy about the art of survival, including the ability to read a map and utilize a compass.

"Your life will depend on it," the recruits were told over and over.

To illustrate the point, small groups of Marine recruits were taken out of their barracks blindfolded and placed in a helicopter and taken for a ride. No information given as to their destination. The helicopter made many turns to confuse the recruits and to avoid providing a point of reference. The recruits were given one compass and one map and told to make it back to camp in forty-eight hours.

"Use whatever skills you have learned to survive," was the mantra used by the Marine instructors.

Being dropped in the middle of nowhere was nothing compared to the POW concentration camp simulations. For weeks the Marine recruits were treated like prisoners of war. They were mentally and physically abused but Thomas called it mental training.

"Be prepared for the worst case scenario," was repeated by the Marine instructors, again and again.

Thomas was surprised when many of the Marine recruits did not pass the test. Some panicked and gave up and many asked to be released from service.

It's all about discipline, Thomas would say. You must have discipline to survive anywhere. Thomas never forgot the rigorous weeks of training at Camp Pendleton.

The last sixteen weeks were spent in Battalion School, in the motor pool. Thomas was part of group responsible for fueling the machinery and vehicles used at the camp. After boot camp and infantry school, the motor pool was a welcome change of training. Thomas loved it because he got to play with tractors and forklifts.

The next stop was Okinawa. The legal paperwork and vaccination shots required three days. Then it was Da Nang, Vietnam. The in-country-briefing was a formality, they all knew about proper behavior in a foreign country.

"You represent the United States, so please behave in a proper manner and do not embarrass your country," the officers said.

Everybody was sent to different places after they got to Da Nang. It was done in accordance with their training in Battalion School. Tom's final destination was Dong Ha, working with heavy machinery. He met Samuel Anderson there. Both were young and scared to death. Ten days after his arrival in Vietnam, Thomas was told by his commanding officer to check out his gear. He was going out on patrol.

Every single conscript did his best to prepare himself for combat. They made mental notes during training camp; they pictured themselves in difficult situations; they formed a plan of attack; and so on and so forth. But nothing can capture the fear a recruit feels when he's told to get ready for patrol. Thirteen soldiers set out on patrol. The first two hours passed without an incident. And then, without warning, the fighting started. Shots came from everywhere. Tom's instincts took over; in seconds he was on the ground, crawling, taking cover, watching the exchange of gunfire take place.

Everything appeared to move in slow motion, the shots, the yelling, the small traces of fire, and the smoke coming from the weapons. It was chaos.

Then, as if propelled by a tempest, the fire fight picked up velocity.

He didn't know who or what to shoot at.

Shit!

The worse part was the jungle; it was green everywhere!

The jungle engulfed him. He was confused. There was no sense of direction. Where is the fucking enemy?

Quickly, Tom became aware of sweat running

down his face and the smell of sweat under his shirt, the bitter taste of bile in his mouth, and the soaring heat of the jungle. His vision became a blur, obscured by sweat and fear. More out of fear then skill, Tom started shooting in different directions. When he stopped to reload, he saw a figure moving in the distance. He took a deep breath to gain his concentration. A Vietnamese was shooting at them, taking refuge behind a tree trunk. Tom waited, aimed, and when he saw an opportunity, pulled the trigger.

After firing the shot, time stood still, and with immense clarity, Tom saw the impact of the bullet. The shirt of the Vietnamese moved as the bullet entered and then exited the body. The Vietnamese fell and Tom knew he had killed him. And just as it had started, the fighting quickly ended. The whole place became silent.

The stillness continued for what seemed like an eternity. Nobody did or said anything. His heart was racing and his mouth was dry.

I just shot and killed another human being! He told himself.

His mind was in a miasma, the brain's wiring mechanism misfiring, unable to process information. He was still on his knees when he became aware of a low thumping noise. When he looked down, he saw his hands shaking, the M-14 hitting his lap. He gripped his weapon tighter, trying to stop the shaking, but he couldn't.

A loud voice came to him, "Peterson, pull yourself together! You are fine!" He looked up and saw the commanding officer talking to him.

"This is a war and we have a job to do. You killed the enemy! He was your enemy—do you understand that? It was either you or him! Now pull yourself together and let's go. Let's move out!"

The shaking lasted for almost two hours.

It was during this period that Thomas discovered the paradox of life. It wasn't the weapons training or the survival skills he was learning that made him uncomfortable, but the essence of knowing that under the guise of undeclared war, he had been trained in how to take another man's life. Along with thousands of others, he was sent to fight people he had never met before, people who had caused him no harm. He had traveled thousands of miles to meet the enemy in a far away land, away from American soil. And all because politicians declared that this small country posed a threat to national security. It was better to stop Communism now, before it spreads like a virus. It was a war of good versus evil. Thomas was beginning to understand life was a trade-off. In order to get something, you had to give up something. He needed the Marines to move out of Arkansas and get a college education. The Marines needed him to fight their war. It was a fair trade, for now. He learned something else: when trading, it's best to bargain from the stronger position. Always.

Twenty-three

Carlsbad, California
Monday December 21, 2009

Javier and David were having a late lunch at a restaurant located along Carlsbad Boulevard. From their table they had a clear view of the ocean and the waves moving gently towards the beach.

The day had been a mixture of luck and common sense. After finding Tom's address they only waited about an hour before Tom walked out of his house. He got into his vehicle and drove south towards Interstate 5. Once on the freeway he drove south to downtown San Diego, parked at a public parking lot and got on the San Diego to Coronado ferry to meet the banker.

After the meeting, Javier and David drove north to Encinitas. When they got to Tom's house they drove around the block once, hoping to get a glimpse of Tom or his vehicle parked in the street.

No sign of both. They decided to eat and relax. After dark they would go back to Tom's house and wait there until he made the next move.

Twenty-four

Vista, California
Monday December 21, 2009

For the first time in a long time, Chino had a restless night. He knew something was terribly wrong. The intense interrogation by the gray-haired American agent at the restaurant in Mesa de Otay last Saturday night caught him by surprise, and the visit by the same American and his fat creepy friend yesterday was frightening. The fat guy with a pony tail scared the hell out of him because every time he got rough with Julia, the son of a bitch took pleasure in it. When he was slow answering the questions from the gray-haired man, the fat guy pulled Julia by the hair and slapped her. And for the pleasure of it, he grabbed and squeezed Julia's breasts a couple of times.

"Do they know I have some information about them or are they just guessing?" Chino asked himself. "Am I being set up?"

As a precaution and for his own protection he decided to organize his prized possessions. The 900 grams of cocaine he owned was placed in a large plastic bag. He went out of the trailer and followed the path leading to the storage shed in the back area of the avocado orchard. The storage shed contained fertilizer sacks, tools, small machinery and various bags and plastic containers full of pest control chemicals. Inside the shed he picked up a half-used sack of fertilizer marked with a red tag. He opened the sack and carefully placed the cocaine bags inside. The sack was closed and returned. There was another fertilizer sack marked with a blue tag. The sack had cash inside, almost $20,000 dollars. He removed the money and returned the sack. From a fertilizer sack with a green tag he removed a clear plastic bag. Inside the bag were three computer floppy disks and a folder with information given to him by Mario, his former friend and supplier.

Chino recalled Mario talking nonsense about the thousands of dollars he was going to make, a girl for every day of the week, and a mansion someplace in Tijuana. According to Mario, the floppy disks had information about federal drug agents and Border Patrol agents from the Temecula and Otay Mesa Border check points on the take. Tony gave Chino the three floppy disks for safekeeping.

Chino was not stupid; he had a feeling the agents weren't done with him. He was going to visit Frank tonight and tell him everything he knew about the agents, the cash and the cocaine. Even though Frank knew Chino was involved in illegal activities, he never criticized him or looked down on him. Chino trusted him.

Twenty-five

Vista, California
Monday December 21, 2009

It had been a good day. Frank collected the paperwork for the last two jobs, placed them in separate manila folders and called John's office and set up an appointment with Margaret, the office manager. Frank drove to the Oceanside office and delivered the two folders. After inspecting the invoices, Margaret issued Frank a check. On his way home he stopped at his bank and at the Albertsons market. He bought groceries for the rest of the week and various household items. At home he had a vegetable salad and a grilled cheese sandwich for dinner with a bottle of water, instead of a beer. Frank proudly noticed forty-eight hours had passed without reaching for a beer or a cigarette. After watching the late news on CNN he went to bed and had fallen fast asleep.

Sometime before midnight, the sound of car tires rolling on the lose gravel leading to Frank's trailer increased as the vehicle got closer. When it reached the trailer the car stopped and the engine was turned off. The driver emerged from the vehicle. Cautious, she walked up to Frank's trailer, opened the screen door and knocked on the door. The first couple of solid knocks woke Frank up. The next two knocks startled him.

"What the hell." Frank said to himself, as he tried to find his bearings.

Two more solid bangs came from the door. "I'm coming!" Frank yelled to the door. He got up and stood by the door, frozen by fear. He wore shorts and a T-shirt.

"Frank! Frank! Open up, please!" A woman was yelling.

"Frank, it's me Julia! Open up!" She was turning and pushing on the door knob.

Julia? What the hell is she doing here? Frank checked his watch. It was eleven fifty-five.

More pounding on the door, this time the banging was faster and louder. "Open the door! Please!" He could hear the woman crying.

The sobs from the woman became louder. Frank turned on the porch light and with hesitation opened the door.

When the door opened, the woman standing on the porch covered her mouth with her right hand to muffle her sobs. Her long dark hair was disheveled; on the right side of her head a clump of her hair was covered in what appeared to be fresh blood. Her eyes were clear and fully opened. She lowered her hand from her mouth and stood there for a few seconds, unable to utter any words. Confused and scared, Frank just stood there, looking at Julia, waiting for her to make the next move. With the sleeve of her blouse Julia cleaned her nose and wiped the spit from her mouth. She was not looking at Frank anymore; she was looking at the plastic bag she was holding in her left hand.

Unsure of what to do Frank said, "Please come in; it is cold outside."

She looked at Frank and with a quiet voice she said, "No. Please, we need to get out of here right now. They know where you live and they are on their way."

Frank made a frown, what the hell is she talking about?

"We need to get out of here!" She repeated, this time with a stronger voice.

Frank moved closer to Julia, and using his fingers, moved some of the hair away from her face. She had bruises on the forehead and on both sides of her face. Her bottom lip was swollen. Frank was scared and didn't like the things Julia was saying. "What the hell are you talking about? Where's Chino?"

"Chino told those stupid agents or whatever the hell they are, that you were his best friend and he had given you some material to hold, and also told them where you live. One of the guys beat him up pretty good. I don't know for sure, but I think Chino's dead."

The hair on the back of Frank's neck stood up. His body became numb, consumed by fear.

"Don't just stand there, Goddamn it! We have to leave! If we don't get out of here, they will kill us!" Her voice came out loud, full of fear.

Still confused, Frank went back to his bedroom and quickly put on his jeans, socks and work boots. He picked up his jacket and truck keys. He didn't know what the hell was going on, but Julia's bruised face told him they needed a safe place to rest and talk. He knew the place: the house in Fallbrook where he had had the conversation with John Harrison Friday morning. The house was empty, had electricity, running water and aside from John and the owners, nobody knew its location. From the closet he grabbed a large backpack and quickly stuffed it with extra clothes, towels and toiletries.

Julia was standing in the same spot, her body shaking. She just wanted to get the hell away from there.

Frank grabbed Julia by the arm and led her to the car. "We are going to Fallbrook using Taylor Street and then Santa Fe Avenue, OK? I want you to drive to the liquor store down the road and park your car there. Take everything out of the car and then get in my truck; I am going to take you to an empty house in Fallbrook. OK?"

Julia didn't respond, she just nodded in affirmation. They got into their vehicles and quickly drove away.

Twenty-six

Fallbrook, California
Tuesday December 22, 2009

During the twenty-minute ride to Fallbrook, Frank concentrated on his driving while Julia sat slumped in her seat, head leaning against the window. At the end of Santa Fe Avenue he drove along East Highway 76 and five miles later made a left turn on Mission Avenue. A couple of times he looked in the rearview mirror to check for any vehicles driving along the highway, but there was nobody behind him.

When they arrived at the house, Frank parked the truck in the backyard. Julia was trembling when she got out of the truck. Frank came to her, placed his arm around her shoulders and gently guided her inside the house. The house was dark, but there was plenty of light emanating through the large living room window. They sat on the floor near the large window. Frank removed his jacket, folded it and placed it next to Julia. She lay down and used the jacket as a pillow. As a precaution the living room lights stayed off. In case they were followed, Frank wanted the advantage of seeing them first.

Frank leaned over to Julia and whispered, "I'm going to my truck to get some clothes and other stuff. We need to clean your face and hair. OK?"

Julia didn't answer, she just nodded.

Frank went outside and collected the back-pack, two blankets, a small flashlight and some water bottles from his truck. As he carried the items back to the house he couldn't believe his life had changed with a knock on his door. The things Julia said didn't make sense, starting with Chino being beaten to death. If Chino was dead, Julia had involved Frank in a crime. Now both of them were in serious trouble.

Quietly he went back inside the house and placed the blankets, water bottles and the flashlight next to Julia and headed towards the hallway, away from the living room. Inside the bathroom he turned on the lights, walked to the bathtub, grabbed the bathtub plug and placed it in the drain. He tested the water; he wanted the bath hot. While the water was running Frank removed the extra clothes, towels and toiletries from the backpack and placed them on the sink. When the bath was ready he went to the living room to get Julia.

Julia was resting on her side, her hair covering her face; she had her eyes closed but was not asleep. When Frank got close to her she opened her eyes. Frank grabbed one of her hands and said, "I know you are tired and in pain but you need to clean your face and hair. I fixed you a bath. Come on, I'll help you."

Before Julia sat up Frank removed her shoes and socks. Julia didn't protest; she gradually got up and headed toward the bathroom. Frank was guiding her by the shoulders. When they got to the bathroom they stopped in front of the bathtub. Standing in front of her Frank gently helped Julia remove her blouse and brassiere. There were bruises on her right breast and stomach. Julia was visibly wobbly. As she placed her hands on Frank's shoulders for balance, Frank lightly removed her jeans and underwear. Holding her garments, Frank noticed she had soiled her jeans.

Before letting go of her, Frank said, "Julia, please be careful—the water is hot." Frank kept looking at Julia's eyes for a reaction.

With her head down, Julia didn't respond, only nodded.

Gingerly Julia turned away from Frank, and facing the bathtub, placed her right leg inside the tub. Frank was holding Julia by the waist. With her right hand Julia reached for the bathtub's metal handle. When she was ready, she placed her left leg inside the water. More bruises were on Julia's back, legs and left shoulder. After Julia sat inside the bathtub and found a comfortable position, she leaned her head back and closed her eyes. Frank moved the toiletries from the sink and placed them near the bathtub and said, "I am going to leave you alone for few minutes. The soap, towel and shampoo are right here, and when you are done with your bath, use one of my T-shirts. The pants and shorts are big for you but we can make them fit you. Take all the time you want." After giving the instructions Frank picked up Julia's soiled clothes and the backpack from the floor and waited for an answer.

Julia didn't respond.

Frank walked back to the living room and made a small bed using the blankets and his jacket. He sat on the floor, removed a pencil and a piece of paper from his backpack and using the flashlight he made a grocery list. There was no telling how long they had to stay in the house before calling somebody for help. He waited for Julia to finish her bath. He glanced at the plastic bag Julia had carried to his place: It was covered with grime and red stains.

Sometime later he could hear Julia getting out of the bathtub, drying herself and changing clothes. When Julia came out of the bathroom she looked better: the blood was gone from her hair and the skin on her face had a gleaming appearance. The bruises on her face, however, were still noticeable. Taking small steps she walked towards Frank and unhurriedly lay down on the blankets. Frank adjusted the blankets after Julia had closed her eyes. The T-shirt and pants were big on her but she didn't seem to care. It was after one in the morning and dark outside. Frank was not tired but common sense told him to get some rest. He lay down next to Julia to keep both of them warm but facing away from her; he didn't want to give her the wrong impression, particularly after everything she had been through in the last few hours.

Before daybreak Frank opened his eyes. Without making noise he got up, picked up his truck keys and walked out the door. Julia was sound asleep. He drove along the gravel road for about a quarter of a mile before reaching the street. He made a left turn on Reche Road, a right turn on South Stage Coach Lane and then another left turn on East

Fallbrook Street. The first stop was at the Albertsons supermarket located in a large shopping center. Frank bought bottled water, fruit and snacks. After leaving the supermarket he went into a Mexican Restaurant and ordered two large potato and egg *burritos* and two large cups of coffee.

On his way back to the house he was careful not to drive over the speed limit and constantly checked the rearview mirror for a police vehicle. Frank drove considerably slowly when he turned onto the gravel road. If Julia was still asleep, he didn't to want scare her.

Frank parked in the same spot as before, unloaded the food, and carefully carried it to the living room. Julia was still asleep. He placed the food on the floor next to her. He removed part of the blanket and grabbed her hand and said, "Julia, please wake up." Frank waited for a reaction. "I know you are tired but you need to get up and get something to eat."

Julia's eye lids fluttered.

Frank tried again. "Come on, wake up, I brought breakfast and coffee."

Julia opened her eyes to adjust to the dim light in the room and slowly turned her head. Frank gave her a few seconds to collect her senses. She was tired, sore from the events of last night and probably still scared. Julia turned on her side, and using her arms, slowly got up. Frank guided her towards the wall, by the large living room window. Julia leaned back against the wall with her eyes closed. Her face grimaced when her back touched the wall; her back was still tender. Frank collected the brown paper bag and removed the two *burritos* and gave her one. Julia placed the *burrito* on her lap and using both of her hands pushed herself against the wall to adjust her position. She kept her eyes closed. Frank leaned forward to grab the cardboard drink carrier, and with care he removed one of the coffee cups and placed it on the floor next to Julia. When she was ready Julia opened her eyes. Holding the cup of coffee, Frank removed the lid, waiting for Julia to grab it.

"Be careful, please. The coffee is hot. I added cream and sugar." Frank gave Julia his best smile.

She nodded and tried to smile. She took the coffee cup with both hands and held it close to her mouth. The smell of the coffee revived her senses. She took a small sip of the coffee to savor the taste. And then another. Frank sat next to Julia, mesmerized by the ritual and her attractive profile. Feeling self-conscious he grabbed his cup of coffee, removed the lid and sipped the contents. Julia placed the cup of coffee on the floor, lifted the *burrito* from her lap, unwrapped one end and started to eat, slowly at first and then eagerly. Frank did the same. When Julia was done she placed the empty cup of coffee and trash on the floor, near the brown paper bag and then crawled back to the made-up bed. She turned on her side and covered herself with the blanket. Frank collected the empty containers and trash and placed them inside the brown paper bag. After cleaning up, he walked toward the window and stood there admiring the view: a new day was beginning to emerge, the faint rays of sunlight were breaking through the light mist surrounding the tall trees of the property.

Frank couldn't believe his luck. This type of crime only happened on television shows, like *Law and Order*. Common sense told him Julia was part of a plan gone haywire and she involved him because he was an easy target. But his gut feeling told him otherwise. Julia's tears, bruises and the look of fear on her face were real. But why kill Chino? Frank didn't know. If Julia was being truthful, she was a witness to a crime and he was aiding and abetting her. Right now she needed help. Frank had two choices: call the police right now and have the law take over the crime or help Julia find a way out of this mess.

They needed help but who could he talk to? Maybe calling the police was not a good idea; if the people looking for Julia were federal agents, they can claim jurisdiction over the crime and take over the case. If Julia was right and Chino was dead, they had to do something soon because they both were in serious danger.

Bill Morgan came to mind. Bill was a retired police officer from the city of Oceanside, a Korean War veteran, and an old friend going back to Frank's construction days. They met when Frank landscaped Bill's house.

Frank grabbed his jacket and walked out the door. He got into his truck and drove out of the gravel driveway, heading towards Mission Avenue. The truck followed the avenue south all the way to the town of Bonsall. At the end of Mission Avenue he made a right turn and headed west toward Bill's house in Oceanside.

Twenty-seven

Vista, California
Tuesday December 22, 2009

Julia's daring escape caught Tom by surprise. It worked because Tom was distracted using his cell phone, immersed in a false sense of superiority. Julia hit him on the head; his body tumbled, causing him to hit his head against the wall with great force, knocking him out for couple of minutes. When he came to, he heard the running water coming from the kitchen faucet. He got up, feeling faint. He noticed Sam's body down on the kitchen floor, bleeding from the head. Tom walked to the sink and washed his face with warm water. From a metal rack he grabbed a kitchen towel and dried his face with it. Regaining his composure he ran the towel under the water faucet until it was soaking wet. He bent down over Sam's body and placed the wet towel on Sam's forehead, hoping to revive him. Sam didn't react. Tom wet the towel again and placed it on Sam's neck. Sam reacted by opening his eyes. Tom told him to stay down; he had been hit on the head, knocked out and probably had a concussion. Taking his time Sam sat up, eyes glazed. Tom gave him the towel and told him to clean his face and remove the blood from his hair.

Later they sat at the kitchen table. The girl complicated their plan by getting away and taking Sam's flashlight and jacket with a set of keys inside one of the pockets. The flashlight had Chino's and Sam's blood on it. Their egos created a weak spot the girl took advantage of. Things were getting out of hand, and it was Tom's responsibility to rein everybody in.

Tom was the leader. The reason for years of success was simple: the group had a purpose. It started with a discrepancy on the part of Stewart, the investment adviser. Stewart committed multiple felonies by spending millions of dollars entrusted to him by investors on personal trips to Las Vegas, gambling on college and professional basketball games, and living a high life he couldn't afford. Scared out of his mind, Stewart came to Sam for help; they had known each other since high school.

Sam had to restrain himself while listening to Stewart's bullshit story. How the hell can anyone blow millions of dollars and not expect to get caught? Stewart cried the entire time, pleading with Sam to help him. Stewart said he would rather kill himself than go to jail. Sam's initial response was: *where the fuck do you think I can get millions of dollars?* Then added: *Maybe I can use my debit card and get it from an ATM machine?*

Sam could have said no to his friend, but there was a voice inside his head saying, maybe if I help Stewart, I can also help myself. After drinking a couple of beers, Sam thought about Tom. Both had attended a weapons training in Calexico, the small town by the Mexicali border, and hit it off right away. Although Tom had an outstanding reputation within the San Diego branch of the DEA, he was also openly critical of government, particularly lobbyist, overrated politicians and the U.S. foreign policy.

When Sam met with Tom, he couldn't tip-toe around the issue of buying and selling drugs for a profit. He explained Stewart's predicament, and had expected Tom to be at least superficially shocked and offended. But Tom showed no emotion. He said yes right away, and within twenty-four hours, a plan was devised. The idea was simple: use drug money stored in the evidence warehouse in Chula Vista as seed money, and then purchase cocaine from Tom's contacts in Tijuana or Playas de Rosarito. Sam's job was to allow the vehicles transporting the cocaine to pass across the Otay Mesa and Temecula check points. The agreement was to deal in small quantities involving manageable amounts of money. With each transaction Stewart would replace portions of the missing funds. The drug deals were done at random to avoid suspicion from other agencies looking at drug trafficking along the border. Each completed deal brought a sense of euphoria. It was a chess game: they matched wits against other agencies and they won each time.

When the funds were replaced, Stewart invited a few of his business acquaintances, as well as Tom and Sam, to the Torrey Pines Country Club for a dinner celebration. At the country club Stewart was in his element: he was not the timid banker working for a Del Mar high power brokerage firm; he was a wealthy investor enjoying the fruits of his labor. Fueled by expensive meals and imported wine, Stewart made speeches about luck, opportunity and smarts being the keys to financial investment and financial freedom. Between speeches and glasses of wine it became clear to Tom they had bailed Stewart out of his quandary and given him back his legitimacy, but at his own and Sam's expense. After making money for their friend, what did Tom and Sam have to show for it? Now that

Stewart had been reinstated as a legitimate investment wizard, why not let Tom and Sam enjoy some of the same rewards?

Stewart was reluctant to participate, afraid his luck might run out and his life as an investment genius might come crumbling down. Tom and Sam promised a few deals, and they were out. The temptation and the thrill of the chase became addictive. Like an alcoholic at a party announcing he was going to check himself into rehab but failing to give an exact day. The money was intoxicating on many levels: it provided luxuries, women and power. Wealth gave them a false sense of security and Tom knew it, but he failed to act on it. Arrogance led to complacency, allowing Sam to become idle and succumb to temptation. It was a matter of time before the police on either side of the border became suspicious of their activities and started to track them down. It was time to clean up the mess and then go home.

Without a prelude, Tom said, "I'm sure the girl went to see Frank, the construction guy Chino mentioned. I don't believe the girl is smart enough to call the police. Let's go to Frank's house, find them and bring them back here. I will talk to them and when we are done, you can go home. I will take care of the rest. But I need you in control; I don't want you to fuck this up and make this mess bigger than it already is. Sam—tell me you understood everything I just said to you?"

During Tom's discourse Sam had been listening while applying pressure to the cut he had on the left side of his head. When Tom asked the question he slowly nodded in agreement.

Tom knew Sam's pride and ego had been severely wounded. That was why he had readily agreed to Tom's plan. "Sam, I need you to stay focused and concentrate on what we need to do. Don't fuck things up by making this personal. The girl outsmarted us; it's that simple. One more time: don't fuck things up."

Sam kept cleaning his cut, avoiding Tom's gaze, looking down at the table pretending to listen to the sermon. He finally looked at Tom, and without uttering a word, nodded in agreement.

"Let's move Chino's body and dump it somewhere in the middle of the avocado orchard. Before we leave we need to clean the bedroom and the kitchen. Let's be methodical about this; I want to make sure we remove any item related to us before we leave, including the towel you are holding."

After rolling Chino's body in a ravine and covering it with dry tree branches, and cleaning all the blood traces from the bedroom, living room, and kitchen, both got into Tom's car and drove away. They drove west on Ormsby Road and at the traffic light made a left turn onto East Vista Way, heading towards Taylor Street less than four miles away.

Hidden behind tall shrubs was a wine-colored car with Javier and David inside.

On Monday Tom returned to the trailer followed by Sam. The two officers stayed inside the trailer and during that time no vehicles came in or out. David and Javier walked around the trailer and intended to enter and catch Tom or Sam by surprise, but they changed their minds. There was a chance other federal officers were inside the trailer.

Tom and Sam came out of the trailer early in the morning carrying a body into the avocado orchard. Now both of them left the trailer driving one car, a sign they were coming back.

Who was the dead person?

With their weapons drawn, both went inside the trailer. They checked the two bedrooms, the living room, and the kitchen. Both walked back to the car and drove out of the avocado orchard, heading back to Encinitas.

Meanwhile, Tom and Sam searched Frank's trailer. It was empty. They got back in the car and drove on Oceanside Boulevard, straight towards

Oceanside. Before getting on the highway, they pulled into an IHOP restaurant.

They had their first cup of coffee in silence. After the waitress refilled their cups Tom said, "We're tired and need some rest. I am sure the girl is with Frank and both are hiding someplace. They can't go to the police without implicating themselves. Let's go back to my house, get some rest, tend to your head injury, and then return to Frank's trailer tomorrow morning. There has to be an address that shows where they are hiding; we need to go back and carefully check the trailer again, but we need to do it well rested and with clear heads."

Sam nodded in affirmation. His thoughts were someplace else.

He had been embarrassed by a female, a fucking Mexican's bitch. She was going to pay for her mistake and beg for mercy, more than once.

After eating their breakfast, Tom's car pulled out of the restaurant's parking lot, made a right turn and then got on the South Highway 5 ramp.

Twenty-eight

Oceanside, California
Tuesday December 22, 2009

Frank drove on East Cassidy Street and found a parking space in front of Bill's house. After locking the truck he walked up to the house and knocked on the front door. Bill opened the door and smiled: he was pleasantly surprised to see Frank standing in front of him. Bill led Frank to the kitchen where he served him a cup of coffee. It took them a few minutes to add cream and sugar to their coffees, move past the initial pleasantries, grab a chair, and find a comfortable sitting position at the kitchen table. From Frank's physical appearance and demeanor Bill understood it was not a social visit.

Bill took a sip of coffee. With a pleasant smile he asked, "I haven't seen or talked to you in a long time, my friend. And from where I am sitting, it appears you are carrying all the worries of the world on you shoulders. Are you OK?"

"In a way I am." Frank placed the cup of coffee on the table and rubbed his hands against each other nervously. With a forced smile he added, "I'm fine but I have a friend that needs help."

Bill continued, "OK. Go ahead and tell me why you are here. How can I help you and your friend?"

Between sips of coffee Frank did his best to explain his friendship with Chino; meeting Julia a few years back; Chino's dealing with drugs and bringing girls to migrant camps; the conversation he had with Chino a few days back; meeting the strangers at Chino's place last Sunday; and finally Julia knocking at his door late last night. There was also the possibility of Julia making up the whole story and Frank protecting a fugitive. Frank completed the story by adding the events of that morning, including the bruises on Julia's back and shoulders. During Frank's account, Bill didn't say a word, he just nodded. Both knew the next step was to go back to Fallbrook and have a conversation with Julia. Before doing so, however, Bill cautioned Frank about the legal and criminal aspects of the situation. Once the details of the story were checked and rechecked, if the authorities needed to be involved, Bill would make the call. Everything had to be done within the limits of the law, or he was not going to be involved.

Bill wanted to have an in-depth conversation with Julia, and based on the results, he would make a decision. Frank gave Bill the address of the house in Fallbrook, the nearest cross street and his cell phone number.

Bill grabbed the material he needed for the interview with Julia from a small bedroom that served as an office, and once he was ready he asked Frank to be the lead driver.

Twenty-nine

Fallbrook, California
Tuesday December 22, 2009

Frank drove slowly over the gravel road, past the front of the house and parked in the backyard. Frank waited for Bill by the back door. Bill arrived and parked his car next to Frank's truck. He turned off the engine and then grabbed his gear from the passenger seat. Bill got out of the car, and headed towards Frank carrying a blue backpack with his right hand.

When they walked inside the door of the house, they could see Julia seated with her back leaning against the wall next to the large living room window. She tried to smile when she saw them; she looked pale and tired. When they got close to her, Frank introduced Bill to Julia. Bill knelt down, extended his hand and held Julia's hand for a few seconds.

"Julia, Bill is a good friend of mine, and he's here to help us." Frank used the pronoun us because he wanted Julia to understand he was going to help her through this nightmare.

"Hello, Julia. My name is Bill and I am a retired police officer from Oceanside. I am here to listen to your story, and to do my best to help both of you." Bill was careful with his words; he didn't want Julia or Frank to assume he was there to help without analyzing the details of her story.

"Julia, I know you are tired, but we need to talk about your ordeal. I will audiotape the conversation, and I will probably ask you the same question more than once. Be honest; don't leave anything out, even if it incriminates you. This conversation will take a while; if you need a break, just let me know, and I will stop the conversation. It's routine to ask the same questions over and over; it jars the memory and helps to place the story in its proper order. I will need a couple of minutes to set up the tape recorder, and get paper and pencils. In the meantime, why don't you use the restroom, get some water and anything else you need. When you are ready I'll be in the kitchen."

Julia nodded and said "OK . . . thank you for being here and for helping me." Then she quickly corrected herself, "I mean, thank you for helping us." She slowly got up and headed for the restroom. Minutes later she narrated her story.

Julia described her life prior to meeting Chino. She was born in Oceanside and went to El Camino High School. After high school she wasn't interested in college, even though she was an excellent student. She wasn't interested in getting a job either. She moved out of her parent's house and lived with a trucker in Carlsbad for a while. She got to drink beer, smoke pot and travel the California Coast. After a while the long driving hours got boring. She left the truck driver and moved in with a carpenter from Encinitas. The same story repeated itself for the next few years until she met Chino. She wasn't his girlfriend and she didn't have sex with him, or any of the migrant workers. Chino provided beer, pot and cocaine, and in return, she acted as Chino's trophy girlfriend. Chino said Julia was good for business; she gave him a look of prosperity. Even though Chino was selling illegal drugs, he was fun to be around, and he never forced her to do anything against her will.

She explained visiting Frank's trailer to have a beer and a line of cocaine with him, and leaving the trailer the next day. She corrected herself a few times when she talked about Chino's plan to make money by being a courier for high power guys. She mentioned the computer floppy disks with information on them, implicating Border Patrol guys, a federal agent and other people. At that point she hadn't met anybody connected to any law enforcement agency and she was not really sure whether Chino had incriminating information about anybody. She had doubts about Chino meeting with any of the high-power people he constantly talked about.

Last Saturday Chino had gone to a meeting someplace in Tijuana, supposedly to close a deal. He came back from the meeting disillusioned; he was unsure of the situation he was in, and had wondered if the meeting had been a setup from the beginning. Chino was upset about reaching a dead end with the high power people and having to start all over again someplace else. On Sunday Chino was in a somber mood most of the day and he confided in her that the situation with the agents was not over. He was scared and he asked Julia to stay, thinking that with Julia around the agents would think twice about harming him and wouldn't do something stupid to her. When two guys arrived Sunday afternoon, Chino wasn't surprised. Julia didn't know who they were. One was older, with a crew cut, and arrogant; the moment they arrived he asked questions and gave orders, while a tall, fat guy, with a ponytail, took pleasure slapping Julia and Chino. The older guy wanted the information about the Temecula and Otay Border check points Chino got from Mario. The interrogation stopped when the older guy heard Frank's truck arrive. Chino told them Frank was his friend and was in the construction business. They went outside and saw Frank moving branches around, looking for something. The older guy became suspicious of a construction guy arriving out of nowhere at the same time they did. Chino said Frank was harmless and told them where he lived. The ponytail guy talked to Frank anyway. After Frank left in his truck, both slapped Chino pretty hard. They assumed Frank and Chino had something going on. The older guy grabbed Chino by the neck and called him a lowlife, a fucking illegal Mexican. The ponytail guy tried to unzip Julia's pants. Then he asked her to take her clothes off and have sex with him. She refused. He grabbed her by the hair and slapped her. She responded by kicking him hard in the inside part of his right knee. The ponytail guy released her, and let out a grunt, before falling forward to hold his knee. He was stunned by Julia's reaction. After rubbing his knee he got up. With an eerie smile he got close to Julia and hit her hard in the face. Blood came out of her mouth. Then the older guy told him to stop. They left late Sunday night and warned Chino and Julia to stay in the trailer and not to contact anybody. Later, Chino apologized profusely for placing Julia in a dangerous situation, and admitted he was scared of the federal agents.

On Monday Chino and Julia walked to the storage shed behind the trailer. From a fertilizer sack, Chino showed her the computer floppy disks and explained what information was on them. From another fertilizer sack, Chino pulled out a large plastic bag with a kilo of cocaine inside, and another plastic bag with Chino's life savings: $20,000 dollars. The fertilizer bags were marked with small color tags. They removed the bags with the computer floppy disks and the money. Chino told Julia to give Frank the bags; he would know what to do with them. They devised a plan: the computer floppy disks and the money were placed inside Julia's car. She drove the vehicle down the hill and parked it between queen palms and tall ficus trees. In case something went wrong, one of them could use the car to get help.

The federal agent returned, and this time a Border Patrol person was with him. The new guy had short brown hair and was average height. As soon as they walked inside the trailer, and without an introduction, he told Chino he was going to deport him back to the shithole he came from. Once inside the trailer both got comfortable. The Border Patrol guy removed his jacket and dropped it on a chair, and placed a large green-colored flashlight on the kitchen table. Julia heard the jingle of the keys inside the jacket. They asked Chino the same questions from the day before, and when he hesitated, the Border Patrol guy hit Julia. Each time she was hit, she staggered. Julia cried with each blow, but Chino kept denying he had information. The older guy placed a chair in the middle of the living room and asked Chino to sit there. With a soothing voice he apologized to Chino for hitting Julia, but said it was necessary. They were making sure no damaging information was floating around for someone to use against them. Chino knew it was bullshit, and pretended to go along with them. Chino looked at Julia with a look that said, "We are in trouble, get out of here!" The Border Patrol guy held Chino by the right arm and guided him to the bedroom. The older guy asked Julia to take Chino's place. She knew she was in trouble; the tears started to flow, her hands started to shake and her shoulders sagged. She was sobbing when she heard the first blow coming from the bedroom; it was a hollow sound, like a solid object hitting the arm rest of a sofa, followed by a muffled cry. The sound of the blow seemed to last a long time. The sound of the second blow was short but it smelled of death. She heard a body hit the floor with a heavy thud. Julia lost control of her bladder; she felt the warm urine wetting her pants, the chair and then dripping down her right leg. The Border Patrol guy came out of the bedroom holding a bloody green-colored flashlight. He exchanged looks with the older guy. Calmly, he asked Julia to help Chino get up from the floor, and to lie down on the bed. When she walked into the bedroom Chino was laying on his right side, blood seeping from above the left ear. The blood dripped down behind the ear. It created a large dark, red, stain behind Chino's head. She hugged Chino by the chest and tried to pick him up with no avail. Chino's body was dead weight. It smelled of sweat and blood. Using all her strength, Julia managed to drag Chino to the bed. When Julia came out of the bedroom, she had Chino's blood all over her. Quietly, she walked back to the kitchen and sat on one of the chairs. Julia was scared out of her mind. Chino was dead and she was next. The situation was surreal. She didn't want to die, but how could she get away? To stay alive she had to stay lucid; to plan a way out. As she sat there shaking, an opportunity unfolded. She was at the front of the table; the older guy was slightly to her right, standing less then ten feet away, doing something with his cell phone. To her left was the Border Patrol guy using the sink, washing blood from his hands. On the table was the green-colored bloody flashlight. She could push the older guy with enough force to knock him down, grab the flashlight and hit the Border Patrol guy in the head with it, and then head for the door. It reminded her of being stuck at a busy avenue waiting to make a left turn with hundreds of cars zooming by in both directions. In that situation you wait for a gap between cars, but every now and then, you have to make your own gap. With determination she didn't know she had, she charged at the older man, and using her right shoulder, hit him in the chest with everything she had. The federal agent didn't see her coming. He tumbled backwards until he hit the wall, and then landed face down. She grabbed the flashlight from the table, raised it, and taking one long step toward the sink, landed a blow to the agent's head as hard as she could. It was fast. When the blow landed, he dropped to the floor and hit his head against the linoleum floor. Julia headed for the back door, and as she passed the kitchen table, she remembered hearing keys inside the Border Patrol guy's jacket. Julia picked up the jacket, opened the door, and ran through the back yard, jumping over small plants and long dry branches. She opened her car, threw the jacket in the passenger side and got in. From the ashtray she grabbed the ignition key. She turned the car on, and took off. Three blocks from Frank's trailer, Julia pulled the car over. She reached under the passenger's seat and retrieved the large plastic bag with the computer floppy disks inside. She searched the pockets of the jacket and found a set of keys. Julia dropped them inside the plastic bag. She did the same with the bloody flashlight. Then she drove to Frank's place; she didn't know where else to go. Since Chino had told the agents where Frank lived, it was only a matter of time before they came knocking at Frank's door.

The telling and retelling of the story was exhausting. Bill stopped the tape recorder many times, asking Julia for more details and correcting discrepancies in the timeline. During the question-and-answer session the three of them stood around by the kitchen counter, with Julia pacing back and forth, clutching her hands, adjusting her hair and carefully touching her swollen bottom lip. Frank leaned against the counter, watching, listening to the questions and answers. He was surprised by Julia's courage; it was a hell of an ordeal. Frank was saddened by the death of his friend, Chino.

Bill was all business during the interrogation. When the questioning was over Bill had over three hours worth of testimony from Julia and lots of notes.

After placing the audio tapes, notes, and the bloody plastic bags inside his vehicle, Bill came back inside the house and gave them final instructions. Moving to Julia and smiling to reduce the tension, he said, "Julia, it was a hell of a story . . . I believe you. You're an amazing person, and I can't help but admire your courage."

Julia's eyes got wet. She felt relieved, validated. Frank came and held her, cautiously; he knew she was still in a lot of pain.

"I am going back to my house and make phone calls to people I know," Bill said.

Pointing at Julia he added, "All of us are in serious trouble. You gave me material which incriminates federal agents with abuse of power and murder. If the information on the computer floppy disks reveals deals involving drugs, and the transportation of drugs across the border, then it becomes a federal matter involving who knows what agencies. Those guys know you have incriminating evidence about them, and at this point, they want to clean up their mess."

Looking at Frank he continued, "They probably believe you are also involved in this plan, which makes you a target." He paused.

"Here's the situation: are they looking for you? Yes. Are both of you in serious trouble? Yes. Can they kill you for what you know and the evidence you have? Yes." Bill then added, "Frank, how long can you stay here?"

Frank thought about it then answered, "As far as I know, about a week, maybe longer. The construction company that built this house is closed for the holidays and business doesn't start until after the New Year. The owners are from out of town, and I don't believe the house is completely finished."

"That's good, Frank," Bill responded. "This house is better than renting a hotel room. In a hotel, if you go outside they might get lucky and see you. Here you are secluded, away from everybody. I am going back to my house and I'm taking the evidence with me for everybody's protection."

Bill had taken control of the situation without a complaint from Frank or Julia. "If you get caught before I call the proper authorities, don't say anything to these men. Tell them who I am and that I have the evidence they are looking for. Tell them to call me. If we do it this way, both of you are of less value to them, and it adds another number to the equation. They will think twice about killing you because I'm now part of this. They can't call other agencies for help without raising suspicions, or incriminating themselves. And that's what makes them dangerous: they are desperate and unpredictable. I will call people I know, and based on their advice, I will decide what to do next."

Bill walked out the door and got into his car. As he drove around the house, he waved. Standing at the front door, Frank and Julia waved back. When the car was out of view, they sat against the wall by the large living room window. There was nothing else to do but wait. Yesterday Frank was working on his trailer and his personal life had a new start. Now, he was involved with Julia in a crime with incredible complications. If things work out, Julia will probably go to jail, and Frank was out of a job. If everything went according to plan, that is.

They sat next to each other leaning against the wall. Frank grabbed a couple of bottles of water from the floor and gave one to Julia.

Pretending to play with the water bottle label and without looking up, Frank asked, "Why did you come to me?"

Julia thought about her reply. "I wish I could give you a better explanation, but you were the only guy I could think of. Sorry I got you involved."

Frank continued to play with the water bottle label. "Last night when you knocked on the door, I was scared, and when I saw you standing there bleeding, I went numb. I feel stupid right now because I didn't know what to do then, or now. This morning when you were asleep, I thought, why did she come to me? She doesn't know me. But you know what? I'm glad you came to me."

Julia closed her eyes and leaned her head against the wall. "All the things that happened last night and this morning are a blur: from Chino getting killed, me pissing and shitting my pants and everything in between, it's just amazing. Like I said, I'm sorry."

Frank looked at Julia, "I thought about you many times the last few years. I wanted to ask Chino about you, but I was embarrassed because I thought both of you were involved. I assumed you told him about us having a beer at the trailer and me falling asleep and waking up on the floor the next day alone."

Julia kept her eyes closed and tried to smile. "You don't have to explain, I understand. I didn't tell anybody anything; your reputation is safe with me."

Frank smiled. "I'm sorry. I'm acting like a high school kid. Let's change the subject. I'm driving to town to get food. After we eat, let's get some rest.

I'm tired and there is nothing else to do but wait for Bill."

Julia nodded and said, "OK."

Frank got into his truck and drove towards the center of town. At a store he bought a couple of blankets and pillows and from a Burger King he got food. After he parked the truck behind the house Frank sat still. The idea of hiding and waiting for someone else to help them made him feel stupid. He walked back in to the house. Julia smiled when she saw him; her face was still pale and fatigued. Frank sat next to her, opened the bag and gave Julia her food. They ate their food in silence.

As the food was being consumed, Frank wondered why he cared about Julia; they had met only once before, yet, he felt compelled to protect her. Why?

After finishing their meal they spread the blankets and found a comfortable spot. Julia fell asleep first. Frank slept for a couple of hours and woke up. Did he hear somebody walking on the gravel or dream it? Frank glanced at Julia; she was asleep on her left side; he could see her right shoulder gently moving up and down. He crawled towards the front door; when he got near it, he stood up, and with his left shoulder rubbing along the wall, walked towards the window. Even though the day was cloudy he had a good view of the road that led to the house. He stood motionless, looking at the narrow road. There was nobody outside; he was nervous as hell. Depending on somebody else for his safety made him feel powerless.

Frank moved away from the wall and crawled back to Julia. It was difficult to believe he had had a great conversation with John five days before, right here, in the front yard of this house.

Frank wondered about the possibility of Bill finding a legal solution to Julia's problem. Can Bill make a deal about a dead person, federal officers, murder, corruption, and drug dealings?

The immediate problem was the federal agents. It was only a matter of time before they found them. How long could they hide from the agents? It was hours before he fell asleep again.

The screams were short and loud. Frank sat up. Julia was tossing on the floor, her eyes closed. He grabbed her by the shoulders. "It's OK." Frank whispered.

Julia sat up; knees close to her chest, her arms around her legs. She was trembling, sobbing, and rocking back and forth. Cautiously, Frank placed his right hand on her right forearm and when she didn't resist, he held her left hand with both of his hands. He got closer and placed his left arm around her shoulder. She leaned her head against his shoulder. Her trembling subsided. Frank gently lay back down on his pillow, bringing Julia close to him. Minutes later both were back asleep.

Many hours later Frank woke up and quietly walked out of the house. He drove to the near-by Mexican restaurant to buy coffee and food. As much as he tried, he couldn't get some nagging questions out of his mind. What if the federal agents show up right now? Or the homeowners drive up unannounced?

When he walked back to the house Julia was still asleep. He placed coffee near her. Using both hands he removed the lid of the cup of coffee. The smell of coffee began to permeate the living room. Frank sat back against the wall and started drinking his coffee. The aroma roused Julia from her sleep. It was still early in the morning; outside the weather was cold but with clear skies.

Julia opened her eyes and stayed motionless for a few seconds. She moved the blankets away and sat up. She reached into her pants pocket, pulled out a rubber band and using both hands fixed her hair in a pony tail. Frank pointed to the cup of coffee on the floor next to her. Julia reached for the cup. Frank got closer and said, "The coffee is hot."

Julia smiled and said, "It smells great. Thank you."

Frank replied, "You are welcome."

There was still an aura of awkwardness, but not as uncomfortable as before. Julia looked rested and with more energy. After she finished her coffee she stretched her arms wide, trying to bring energy into her body. She stretched one more time and then hugged herself.

She smiled. "Thank you again for the coffee. It tasted fantastic."

"It was my pleasure. I also got breakfast for both of us." From a plastic bag Frank removed the Mexican food and placed it next to her. He got closer and said, "I don't want to be dramatic, but I want to talk about an action plan in case Bill can't help us. But we have plenty of time. First let's eat."

Julia said, "Thank you for everything." Taking a deep breath she continued, "You are right. We need to talk about this . . . mess."

Thirty

Vista, California
Wednesday December 23, 2009

After many hours of much needed rest, Tom, with an ill-tempered Sam in tow, walked out of his residence oblivious to the morning's traffic and flow of pedestrians. Both got into Tom's car. With ease, the vehicle headed north on Cornish Drive, made a right turn on East F Street and headed straight towards freeway 5. They drove back to Vista in silence; there was nothing they hadn't discussed already.

Thirty minutes later the car parked in front of Frank's trailer. They were unafraid to be seen, and determined to find the girl and Frank as soon as possible. Frank was in the construction business, which meant there was an address or a phone number inside the trailer.

After inspecting the kitchen they moved to the bedroom. There was nothing on top or under the bed; the dresser drawers had T-shirts, underwear, socks and other pieces of clothing, but no files. No documents in the bedroom closet, either. When Tom sat on the bed he noticed the bed had a hard frame. He pulled up the bed cover and sheets. The wooden bed frame had four drawers. In one of the drawers was a folder with copies of receipts for material purchased for a house in Fallbrook. The dates on the receipts were recent.

Grinning, Tom said, "The girl and Frank are hiding in Fallbrook," holding the folder he added, "I have the address."

Sam smiled, thinking, "Get ready, bitch, I'm coming after you."

Holding the folder, Tom walked out of the trailer followed by Sam. They got inside the car and headed towards Fallbrook. Energy was flowing through Tom's body. After an edgy twenty-four hours, he was feeling much better. Once he got Frank and the girl back to Chino's trailer, he was going to tell Sam to get the fuck away. He could do the rest by himself.

As Tom's car moved along East Vista Way and then turned right on Highway 76, the wine-colored Volvo carrying Javier and David was behind them, keeping a safe distance.

Javier and David followed Tom's car back to Vista until it stopped at a trailer off Taylor Street. Grim faced, Tom and the Border Patrol guy entered the trailer. Minutes later both walked out of the trailer smiling, with Tom carrying a manila envelope.

Where are they going and what's inside the manila envelope? David wondered.

Thirty-one

Fallbrook, California
Wednesday December 23, 2009

Frank took a bath first then made a quick trip to a Laundromat to wash the few clothes they had. While Frank was away Julia cleaned the living room and the kitchen, condensing the trash and separating the food they had left. Once she completed the tasks she went into the bathroom to take a bath.

After he returned, Frank knocked on the bathroom door, and placed a clean set of clothes on the floor. He walked back to the living room and stood by the front window, looking at the scenery. It was a wonderful December day with a few small clouds, but mostly blue skies.

Julia came out of the bathroom walked towards the window and stood next to Frank. She stood motionless, looking out, immersed in the beauty of the landscape. Frank looked at her profile. She was as attractive as he remembered her; the kiss they shared at his trailer many years ago flashed through his mind.

Looking at her he said, "I'm sorry to spoil this moment, but if you are ready, let's talk."

She kept her eyes on the landscape. Then she turned and said, "I'm ready."

"I don't know how much Bill can help us. How much can he do without involving the authorities? Chino was killed, and anyway we look at it, the police will investigate. We only have two choices: the authorities get involved or we move far away. The answer is easy for me because everything I own is here." Frank waited for a response.

Julia had been listening, rubbing her hands nervously. "I'm aware the police or somebody with authority needs to get involved. That means I will have to answer questions about Chino, drugs, his death and other questions that will incriminate me. I know I'm going to jail. Or the possibility of going to jail is there. I don't want to run away either." She waited for Frank's response.

Frank took a deep breath. "I will also face charges. How many? I don't know. At least aiding and abetting. I want to stay here. Shit, this is difficult to explain. When things get settled, when this shit is over, you are welcome to stay with me. Before you knocked on my door, I made serious changes in my life; about my job and lifestyle. Then you came. It sounds like bullshit, but I'm a firm believer that things happen for a reason, and maybe it was karma that we met again. I thought about you many times after that kiss in the trailer. But I don't believe it was meant for us to be together then. Today I have a place of my own; I have control of my life, and I want you to know that whatever happens, I will be waiting for you." Frank paused.

Looking at Frank, Julia said, "I have no money or a place to stay. It's a long story. Maybe we can talk about it someday. And if you want me, I would like to stay with you."

She paused, then corrected herself, "I'm sorry it came out like I had no place to go, and your place is better than nothing."

Frank smiled and said, "I understand. I know what you mean."

"Now let's talk about the agents. They will find us, one way or another, because like Bill said, they are desperate. Chino is dead and we have evidence. They are not going down without a fight. If they find us, they are going to kill us, I'm sure of that." Frank paused to let his words sink in.

Julia didn't answer, she only nodded in agreement.

"They are going to find us. The question is, will they do it before Bill gets here? We can't stay here forever." He looked at Julia. She was back looking outside the window, lost in a trance.

Without turning she responded, "I'm done being a victim. I was scared when they beat Chino to death, but I managed to find the courage to get away from them. I don't know about you, but I'm not ready to die. I'm going down swinging; I will not let anybody kill me like a fucking dog."

"OK," Frank said. He didn't know how to respond; he was taken aback by Julia's reaction.

"I don't know exactly what I am going to say, or do, when I see the men again, but I will think of something. If I start, just follow my lead and vice-versa. Is that OK?" Julia was now looking at Frank.

"That's fine with me," Frank responded. Then he added, "Let's wait one more day. If nothing happens by tomorrow morning, we'll make a decision and go someplace else and do something."

"Fine," Julia said.

"One more thing," Frank said, intently looking at Julia. "Let's be ready in case they show up here."

Julia took a deep breath and nodded.

They were tense, eager to get things moving, but there was nothing to do but wait for Bill's phone call.

They sat back in the living room, leaning against the wall and talked about Frank's job, but in general terms. Serious conversations had a tendency to drain energy, and neither one was in the mood for that.

The faint noise of a car approaching set off an alarm in Frank's brain. He got up and moved to the edge of the window. Before the car came into view, the sound of the car approaching was unfamiliar. It wasn't Bill's car. Adrenalin pumped into his veins. Whose fucking car was it? Julia came to the window, with fear imprinted on her face. She was stunned to see Tom and Sam arriving. She had anticipated their arrival but not this soon. Frank grabbed Julia by the arm and said, "Let me do the talking, but be ready to move or run."

Julia nodded and said, "I'm OK." She was taking deep breaths to calm herself.

From the window Frank nodded to Tom and Sam as their vehicle passed by. It was a message: I'm not intimidated. Looking at Julia he said, "Try to stay behind me."

Julia was afraid, but she wasn't going to show it. They heard the doors of the car open and then close. One set of footsteps moved to the front door. One person stayed in the back. Frank and Julia remained in the middle of the room, looking towards the back and front doors.

Slowly the doorknob of the front door started to turn. The door was pushed open. Nobody came in. The backdoor opened and somebody entered the house.

Tom, holding his 9mmGlock in his right hand, checked behind the door. There was nobody there. He closed it with his left hand. Sam, also holding a Glock, came in from the front door. Tom motioned Sam to check the bedrooms. Sam walked past Frank and Julia without looking at them.

"You don't have to check the rooms; there's nobody else here." Frank's voice came out with authority.

"Thank you for the advice, but we'll make sure ourselves." Tom was looking past Frank, still holding the gun, waiting for Sam to return from one the bedrooms. Sam returned to the living room, and looking at Frank, placed his gun back in his holster. He turned, nodded to Tom, and said, "The house is empty."

Tom let out a sigh and then placed the gun back in his holster. Sam grabbed Julia by the arm and tried to push her towards one of the bedrooms.

With a quick move, Julia pulled back her left arm. And using her right hand pushed Sam's arm away.

"Don't touch me!" Julia yelled. Her voice came out dry and strong. She glared at Sam and held her gaze. I will not let anybody intimidate me anymore, she said to herself.

"You fucking bitch!" Sam took a long step towards Julia, arm raised high.

"Stop it! Goddamn it, stop it!" Tom screamed, walking towards Sam, his face red, nostrils flaring. Before this day is over I am going to kill this bastard! Tom said to himself, as he pushed Sam away from Julia.

"Back off, you son of a bitch! Don't you dare come near me!" Julia was holding her gaze on Sam. She took a couple of steps back and got close to Frank.

It took Tom a minute to compose himself. He was embarrassed; he couldn't believe Sam was willing to compromise the entire situation just to soothe his fucking ego.

Tom looked at Julia and then at Frank. "You don't seem surprised to see us." His voice was calm, back in control.

"We were waiting for you," Julia answered. Frank kept quiet, ready to act.

"OK, then let's get to the point. We need the flashlight and the other material you took from us." Tom got an uncomfortable feeling. The girl seemed too relaxed.

"We have the flashlight with Chino's and that guy's blood on it," Julia pointed to Sam. "We also have floppy disks with information related to both of you; we also have my blouse with Chino's, and that guy's, blood and mine on it." Smiling, Julia pointed to Sam. "And don't forget, I am also a witness to Chino's murder."

Holding Frank's arm she continued, "The evidence you want is not here. Somebody else has it and you are not going to get it back that easy."

Frank just nodded; he was fine with Julia in control.

Tom ran out of patience. "Let's cut the bullshit: who has the information?"

Before Frank had a chance to answer Julia said, "His name is Bill, he lives in Oceanside and he's a retired police officer."

Taking a step closer, Tom said, "I don't give a fuck who or what he is; I want everything back." Tom wasn't sure. Are they bluffing? He continued, "Let's make this simple; I want everything back now. He either brings the objects to us now, or I will kill you." Looking at Julia, Tom added, "By now you know what Sam is capable of." Tom reached inside his jacket and took out a cell phone. He flipped the cell phone open and tossed it to Frank.

Frank caught the cell phone, unsure of what to do with it.

"Call Bill and tell him to bring the evidence to Chino's trailer in one hour. If he's one minute late, I will kill both of you. Place the call and then use the speaker phone so all of us can hear. Make the call."

Frank dialed Bill's phone number and then pressed the speaker phone button. Bill answered the phone on the second ring.

"Bill, this is Frank. There are two men here asking for the material we gave you. They said they need the objects in one hour. They want you to come to a trailer in Vista." Frank held the phone, waiting for an answer.

"From the sound of your voice the phone you are using is on speaker mode. I know they can hear me, but tell them I will be there in one hour. What's the address?" Bill sounded calm and Frank didn't know what to make of that.

"The trailer is inside an avocado orchard. Once you get to Ormsby and head towards Interstate 15, take the second dirt road on your right and follow it to the end until you see the trailer," Frank said, and then waited for a response.

"I'll be there. But tell the agents you are not driving back with them; I want you to drive your truck back with Julia. One of the guys can ride with you. You drive back in your own truck or there is no deal." Frank looked at Tom waiting for a response. Tom nodded in affirmation.

"They said yes, Bill."

"Then see you soon. Say hello to Julia." Frank closed the lid of the phone and tossed it back to Tom.

Before leaving, Frank and Julia collected all their belongings and the trash that had accumulated during their two-day stay. Tom and Sam didn't interfere with the cleaning, they kept their distance.

When they were ready Tom asked Sam to drive the car back to Vista; he was riding back with Frank and Julia. Tom had a bad feeling. The conversation with Bill had been too easy, and Sam was still a huge problem. Even though they had talked about being professionals and sticking to their plan, Sam was blinded by revenge. As soon as it was safe, he was sending Sam home. The bastard had become a liability.

After following Tom and Sam to Fallbrook and parking at a safe distance, Javier and David knew one of them had to get out and find the reason why Tom and Sam had driven to that address. They were taking a risk because the street was deserted, and their vehicle was the only one parked out on the street. If Tom and Sam came out of the driveway and made a left turn towards downtown, they were going to be exposed. After waiting a couple of minutes David got out and walked a short distance along the sidewalk, followed the dirt road for a few yards and then took cover behind the trees. He continued walking, doing his best to stay low. He found a place close to the house and a safe distance from the dirt road. From his position he saw the girl from the trailer in Vista and another person carry plastic bags and other things to a truck.

What's the girl doing here? And who's the other person?

He called Javier and gave him the information.

David saw Sam driving the lead car, followed by the truck with Tom, the girl from the trailer, and the unknown man. He called Javier again, and told him to wait until the cars were out of sight, and then to come and pick him up. David wanted to check inside the house, but there was no time. As soon as he saw the Volvo drive into the gravel road, he walked out from behind the trees to meet the car. He opened the passenger door and quickly got inside.

"The girl got away Monday, which is why we didn't see her come out of the trailer Tuesday with Tom and Sam," David said, adjusting the seatbelt.

"Now it makes sense. They checked the trailer twice: yesterday and today, because they were looking for an address," Javier said, keeping his eyes on the road.

"They found the address today. But how the hell did she get here?" David asked.

"She must know the person driving the truck. When she got away, she probably went to see him, and he brought her here," Javier added.

"Why not kill both of them back at the house? The place is secluded, it would take days to find them," David wondered.

Javier said excitedly, "Because the girl knows something about these guys or has something that belongs to them!"

Things were neatly falling into place. Right now it was a sure bet both vehicles were returning to the trailer hidden in the avocado orchard, back in Vista.

Thirty-two

Vista, California
Wednesday December 23, 2009

Sam arrived first, and after parking the car, waited a moment before getting out. The trailer was dark. He removed the gun from his holster and held it in his right hand. Keeping his eyes on the front door, he got out. He stood in place for a few seconds, listening, but there was nothing out of place. The trailer and its surroundings were silent.

Frank arrived and parked his truck next to Sam's car. The ride from Fallbrook had been quiet; nobody uttered a word. Frank noticed Tom pulling his gun from its holster and placing it inside the right pocket of his jacket.

I am not ready to die, Frank said to himself.

The three of them got out of the truck and headed towards the trailer. Julia turned pale and felt sick before she got to the front door. She didn't want to go inside and revisit Monday night's events. Frank moved next to her and held her by the left arm. Leaning over he whispered, "It's OK. You can do this."

Julia didn't respond; she only nodded in affirmation.

Tom ushered Frank and Julia in, but waited a few seconds before entering himself. He reached for the gun inside his jacket pocket and glanced around, making sure they were not being followed.

Javier drove the Volvo past the dirt entrance leading to Chino's trailer on purpose. He kept driving until he got close to the Interstate 15 on-ramp, pulled into the ARCO gas station and then turned back on Ormsby Street. They decided to wait before driving in and parking behind the tall bushes again, in case other people showed up.

Right now, only Tom and Sam and two other people were inside the trailer. Both were manageable and they were certain the girl and the truck driver would not interfere.

On the way back the Volvo turned in, and slowly moved along the dirt road, and then parked in the same spot as the day before. Javier and David decided to wait; there was always the possibility of more people coming in for a visit.

They were right.

A moment later, the headlights of another vehicle came into view. The car moved slowly, placing Javier and David in a predicament. At that speed there was a good chance the driver would see them inside the car and assume they were part of the scheme unfolding inside the trailer. Quickly, both got out, moved behind the car, and hid behind tall shrubs.

When the car went by, David picked himself up and quickly crossed the narrow dirt road and positioned himself behind a large boulder with a clear view of the trailer and the cars parked by the front door.

Bill parked next to Frank's truck, turned off the engine and waited for somebody to come and greet him. He knew somebody was outside waiting his arrival. He noticed the car parked at the entrance, hidden behind the tall plants.

Tom emerged from the left side of the trailer, pointing the gun at Bill. With the gun he motioned for Bill to get out of the car and go inside the trailer. Taking his time Bill opened the door of the car and got out. With slow but steady steps he walked towards the front door of the trailer. Bill opened the door and walked in. He saw Frank first; his face pale, standing by the kitchen table next to Julia, touching one of her shoulders. Julia was sitting in one of the chairs holding a kitchen towel to her mouth. Sam was standing in front of her, a smirk on his face.

Bill walked towards Frank and when he was close to him, he hugged him, and then whispered, "There is a gun under the driver's seat in your truck." He bent down to talk to Julia. He gently moved the kitchen towel away. She had blood on her mouth and there was a bruise on the right side of her face.

"I told that bitch she was going to pay for what she did to me," Sam announced proudly to no one in particular.

Bill didn't react to Sam's declaration.

Placing his weapon back in its holster, Tom said to Bill, "Turn around, open your arms, and spread your legs."

Bill complied with the command, and as he was being searched, he said, "I don't have a weapon or a wire, if that's what you are concerned about."

After being searched Bill moved back and stood next to Frank and Julia.

Looking at Bill and Frank, Tom pointed to the kitchen chairs, "Both of you take a seat."

Bill and Frank complied with the command. Smiling, Tom removed the gun from his holster and pointed it at Frank's head. "All right, Bill, where the fuck is the evidence?"

From Bill's demeanor, Tom knew he was in trouble. He was sure Bill didn't bring the material because he was planning to bargain with him. Fuck!

Looking at Bill, Tom spoke again, "I'm tired and I want to go home, Bill. Where is my stuff?"

Without showing any emotion Bill got up from his seat and replied, "I don't have your information with me. Did you really believe I was going to bring the evidence to you, to a place far away from people, so you guys can kill us? Be serious. The evidence Julia gave me are with the San Diego Police Department; they know who you are and what you are doing. It's only a matter of time before they come looking for all of you."

Walking towards Julia, Tom said, "I guess you didn't take me seriously when I said we were going to kill them if you failed to bring my computer disks and other material. I believe you need a demonstration, Bill." He grabbed a handful of Julia's hair, and then pulled her face up.

Julia didn't utter a word but the grimace on her face said it all.

Taking a risk, Bill walked a couple of steps towards Tom and said, "Who are you people? You are a federal officer, yet you've killed the person that lived here. Both of you represent the law. Then you break that trust by dealing in drugs like common criminals. And now, abusing your authority, both of you severely beat this poor girl. Why?"

Letting out a sigh Tom answered, "I don't have the time or the motivation to give you a lecture on ethics right this minute, old man; maybe we can have coffee some other day and talk morals and other bullshit. Besides, black people like you wouldn't understand how the real world works."

Bill didn't give up. "I was a soldier in Korea and a police officer once. And never in my career as a police officer did I take anything that I didn't earn or didn't belong to me. What gives you the right to kill and hurt people just because things don't work out for you?"

Visibly annoyed, Tom replied, "Because I can, Goddamn it! It's that simple!"

Bill smiled and asked, "No, there is more to it than that. You took an oath to defend the laws of this country and yet, here you are, in a serious predicament. Are you mad at the government? Were you passed over for a promotion? Did you lose your savings, your investments, or your retirement funds, in the stock market debacle?"

Tom let out a laugh and then paused, "You got to be fucking kidding me, old man. I wasn't passed over for a promotion, and I'm not mad at the government. In fact, I am grateful for the job I have. Let me share something. From the president on down, everybody uses their political position and influence to make money. That's what politics and life are about: money and power. Money gives you a title that separates you from the lowlifes, the scum of this earth. If you go through life, and you don't take advantage of the opportunities that come your way, you are fucking stupid. I'm doing the circle of life: I'm only doing what my predecessor did, and what my replacement will do when I'm gone."

Bill quickly replied, "You can laugh all you want, but not everybody is interested in power and money."

Tom's face became serious. Returning the weapon to its holster he said, "Are you fucking stupid? You actually believe in the 'I'd rather be poor and happy, than rich and sad,' bullshit?"

"Yes I do," Bill said with a hint of a smile on his face.

Looking Bill in the eyes, Tom said, "You care about the 'One nation under God, indivisible, with liberty and justice for all,' lies the government is feeding you every day?"

"Yes," Bill answered again, with more determination.

"You must be fucking kidding! You actually believe you went to Korea to defend the poor people of the south against the evil Communist government of the north? You believe MacArthur was a war hero, a courageous leader, a general loved by his troops?"

"Yes, I do."

"Well, let me enlighten you, old man: MacArthur fucked up because his ego was too big and heavy to carry. His fucking mistakes cost thousands of lives. Soldiers died a brutal death in the snow and those soldiers were sons, husbands, friends and neighbors. But you know what the amazing part was? MacArthur got fired by President Truman for being incompetent, but the son of a bitch died a hero. Can you believe that shit? I am a Viet Nam veteran. In my tour of duty I saw lots of people die, some were friends and some were strangers. Over fifty-thousand people died, thousands became homeless and God only knows how many committed suicide and thousands more are roaming the streets today in need of psychiatric care. Tell me, Bill, why did those people have to die? Freedom? Democracy? It was bullshit! It was business and conquest, Bill. War produces money and Viet Nam was just another piece of land we wanted to take away from the Communists. It was the same situation in Korea. Somebody sitting in the Oval Office makes an executive decision and off we go to a foreign country to die without questioning the reason."

Not knowing where the discussion was going, Sam interrupted the conversation,

"Tom, this isn't the time for a conversation with this guy. Everything he's saying is bullshit. He didn't call the police. He's bluffing. I say let's kill everybody and then get the hell out of here." He paused. And when Tom didn't say anything, he added, "But before we do it, I want to fuck that bitch first. I'm taking her into the bedroom. Keep everybody here." He pointed the gun at Julia and waved it. "Come with me, baby. I guarantee you will enjoy it."

Julia recoiled, fear stamped on her beaten face.

Frank moved and stood in front of Julia. He was scared, afraid of getting shot. He opened his mouth, but nothing came out. His mouth was dry; the tongue felt glued to the roof of the mouth.

Sam turned and pointed the gun at Frank. With abhorrence in his eyes he said, "Get on your knees and beg for your life, you piece of shit!"

With a calm voice Bill said, "Please don't do anything stupid."

"You are calling me stupid? Who has the gun? No wonder blacks are fucking losers. You want to be a hero? Fine, I'll grant your wish."

For a split second Tom contemplated killing everybody in the room, including Sam, but decided against it. "Put the gun away, Sam. I will take care of everything. Go home."

Sam stared at Tom, hesitating.

Tom held Sam's stare, "You are not shooting, or fucking, anybody. The group is getting to you, and that's not good. You need to go home to your family. Please leave."

"I'm not going anywhere without my flashlight and car keys. That bitch is going to give them to me." Sam was still agitated, still holding the weapon in his right hand. You could almost hear the adrenalin flowing through his veins.

"Sam, if you are going to stay, I want you to relax. Please put your gun away." Tom was doing his best to diffuse a situation ready to explode.

Sam looked at Julia and then at Bill. His breathing became less laborious, and his appearance seemed more relaxed.

"Why don't you go outside and get some fresh air. Go outside, relax for a couple of minutes, and then come back." Tom needed Sam out of the way so he could concentrate on Bill.

Sam placed his gun back in his holster and walked out of the trailer.

Looking at Sam closing the front door, Bill said, "Thank you. He could've shot one of us."

"I didn't do it for you, or anybody else. I needed him out so we can finish our conversation and then go home." Tom was beginning to like Bill. He never had a philosophical conversation with a black man before, and from Bill's responses, he seemed like a smart black man.

"You know what, Bill? You are not bad for a black man," Tom looked at Bill, waiting for a reaction.

Bill remained silent.

"That was a complement, Bill. You are supposed to say thank you."

"You talk about me as if I'm a foreigner, someone from a far away land, unaware of the customs and language of California, or the United States, for that matter." Bill's words came out calculated. He was in control of his emotions. Bill continued, "I'm a citizen of this country, I served in the army and I did it with honor."

"You served in a segregated army, in a losing cause, and with an overrated leader. And what did the army give you?" Tom paused, waiting for Bill to make a comment.

Bill didn't answer.

"I'll answer for you: more segregation. The government baited black people into becoming patriots. And after the war you returned to poverty, with no education and to a government that didn't give a shit."

This time Bill was ready. "I disagree with you. You serve your country with honor because we all have a duty to do so. We don't do it because there is something in it for us. The government is not supposed to take care of us; we are responsible for ourselves."

Tom didn't answer right away; he stared at Bill, thinking, trying to organize his thoughts.

Bill held Tom's stare. "We are the greatest nation in the history of the world and we have the moral responsibility to act and defend those that are being oppressed in any part of the world. It would be immoral not to do so. Are some politicians corrupted? I would be naïve not to believe so. Are they using their political power to accumulate wealth? Some are. But deep down, I truly believe that our leaders do care, and they always plan and analyze every situation before they place our soldiers in harm's way. Unfortunately, soldiers do die in any armed conflict."

With a sarcastic laugh, Tom said, "Goddamn! You are amazing, old man! Under what power do we have the right to invade another country? What gave us the right to invade Granada, Panama and Iraq with impunity? We are accountable to nobody! We rattle our sabers and intimidate those that don't fall in line, or those who threaten our way of life. Doesn't that bother you, Bill? Do you honestly believe that for the last eight years the President, the Secretary of Defense, the Secretary of State, and the rest of the presidential cabinet, get up each morning, and over a cup of coffee, agonize and discuss every issue that afflicts every single soldier and veteran of this nation?"

"Again, I believe in my country; I believe we are responsible for our lives and it's not the role of the government to take care of our needs." Bill's face had not changed expression; he was enjoying the discussion.

"I am surprised by your logic, Bill, particularly coming from a black person. You know that when it comes to civil rights, this country has done a shitty job protecting minorities and yet, you still believe in this nation, in this *E Pluribus Unum* nonsense."

Bill didn't take the bait, "No country is perfect, but I believe all of us can make a difference. I agree, we have a long way to go, but we will get there."

From the corner of his right eye, Bill saw a silhouette moving by the front door. Bill had to make a quick decision. If the person coming inside the trailer was part of this group he didn't need to hide. He was hoping they were good guys. Taking a leap of faith, Bill decided to help the person coming in. With calculated steps, he moved in front of Tom, forcing Tom to concentrate on him and ignore the front door area.

Staring at Bill, Tom continued with the debate, "Bill, tell me how it feels when you get behind a white old lady at the local supermarket, and you are there, standing, waiting your turn to pay for your groceries. And then as a natural reaction, she happens to turn around and notices you, a tall back guy standing right behind her. And again, as a natural reaction, she clutches her purse. She thinks you are going to steal her purse, Bill. How does it feel? Please don't tell me it hasn't happened to you, old man."

Bill paused on purpose. He wanted the person that had come in from outside the trailer to make an entrance.

Holding his gun with both hands, Javier yelled, "Put your hands up!" He headed towards

Bill, aiming the weapon at Tom. Almost at the same time, the front door opened, and Sam appeared, hands tied behind his back, and a piece of duct tape placed across his mouth. He was being guided by David.

Holding his gun inches away from Tom's head, Javier said, "My name is Javier Ortega, and I am a police officer from Rosarito, Baja California. With your left hand take your weapon and using two fingers throw it towards the front door."

When Tom hesitated, Javier said, "Drop the gun or I will kill you right here! Don't play games with me!"

Standing next to Sam, David said, "My name is David Avalos and I am also a police officer from Rosarito."

After Tom dropped the gun by the front door, Javier added, "Mr. Thomas Peterson and Mr. Samuel Anderson, we are placing both of you under arrest. You are being arrested for the deaths of Luis Hernandez and Ramiro Flores, two police officers from Rosarito, Baja California.

Tom started to laugh; he couldn't believe what was happening: two Mexicans had come in, unnoticed, and now one of them just announced he, a federal officer, was being placed under arrest!

David moved behind Sam; his left hand holding the collar of Sam's jacket, his right hand holding the gun. The barrel of David's gun was pressing hard against Sam's shoulder blade.

Looking Tom in the eyes, Javier announced, "It took us over five years to track you down, you son of a bitch, but I want you to know it was worth it," and with that, Javier kicked Tom in the crotch. Tom dropped to the floor, his hands covering his groin. For the first time in a long time, Javier felt relieved.

Still holding Sam by the collar of his jacket, David issued a command, "Get down on the floor with your face down."

Sam hesitated.

With a swift move, David kicked Sam behind the right knee and pushed him forward. Sam hit the floor hard. Before Sam had a chance to react, David took a side step and kicked him hard on the ribs, on the left side of the body. A muffled cry came out of Sam. Quickly he emptied Sam's pants and jacket pockets.

When he was done with Sam, David walked to Tom, still lying on the ground holding his groin, and said, "Place your hands behind your back. Don't play games because I will kick the shit out of you."

Tom did his best to lay on his face, arms behind his back. David quickly tied his hands with plastic ties and then checked the pants and jacket pockets for weapons.

Noticing the look of concern on the girl's face, Javier approached her and said, "We are not here to harm any of you. We came for these guys. We've found them, and now we are leaving, and taking them with us."

Julia started to cry; the feeling of relief was crushing.

Frank's pale face also showed relief. He gently placed his left arm around Julia's shoulder.

Bill said, "My name is Bill Morgan. These guys are federal agents, where are you going to take them?"

Javier answered, "As I said, my name is Javier Ortega, Mr. Morgan. We are taking these two guys back to Rosarito with us."

Bill protested, "Those two guys are U.S. citizens. If they have committed a crime you take them to court and you let the American system do its duty. You can't take them out of the country to face their charges. There is an extradition process, you know!"

"Mr. Morgan, we appreciate your concern but we assure you, these two federal officers are guilty.

And they are going to pay for their crimes, but in our legal system." Javier bent down, grabbed Tom by the right arm and helped him get to his feet. He guided Tom towards the wall and told him to sit against it, facing the group.

Tom complied without protesting.

Bill was not giving up, "Are you sure you are going to take them to court? I have a feeling you are not. If you kill them, you are no better then they are, Mr. Ortega. I don't know what crimes you believe they have committed, but every person deserves his day in court, and in our legal system."

Javier didn't answer, instead he walked towards Julia. He noticed the bleeding had stopped but she still had a look of apprehension on her face. When he got close he said, "I am sorry we didn't get here in time to prevent these guys from hurting you."

Walking to the middle of the room, Javier addressed everybody. "We are taking those guys with us and we only have one favor to ask: please don't call the police. Stay here for a couple of hours and let us go away in peace. We are going back home, and we are not coming back; there is no reason why you should fear us."

Sam was struggling to sit up. But each movement sent an agonizing pain to his ribs.

Holding his gun in his right hand, David kept a safe distance from Tom and Sam.

When Javier stopped talking, Julia leaped from her chair, walked a couple of long steps towards Sam, and planting her left leg on the floor, she used her momentum to kick Sam in the face with her right foot. Sam could only moan.

David looked at Javier. Javier nodded in approval, meaning, let her get even.

Bill didn't get a chance to react.

Julia took a couple of steps back and kicked him again. She repeated the scene, but this time she kicked him in the ribs. She did it a few more times without interference from anybody. Sam's body contorted with each kick. When she stopped, her face was flushed, her body heaving from the physical exertion.

Frank came over and asked, "Are you OK?"

Julia nodded.

Facing Bill, Javier said, "Mr. Morgan, we don't want to tie anybody to a chair in order for us to leave this place. Please give us a couple of hours head start and then do as you please. I respect your opinion in this situation but there is nothing you can do. Please don't do anything foolish."

"The police will find you wherever you go. You can't hide," said Bill.

Smiling Javier answered, "Mr. Morgan, we are not hiding. If you ever visit Rosarito, stay on the main avenue until you find the local soccer field, I live across the street from it. You will find us there every Sunday morning watching our kids play a soccer game."

Javier helped Tom get to his feet, while David dragged a bleeding Sam across the room. Without anybody saying a word they all walked out the door.

Thirty-three

Everyone was too stunned to talk after the Mexican police officers left the room. The silence lasted a few moments. Frank hugged Julia and she hugged him back. Bill came and joined them.

The way the situation ended defied logic. For Frank and Julia, this was an affirmation that the good guys do win in the end; that, when mistakes are made, and you own up to those mistakes, a second chance can be given. They had been given a reprieve, an opportunity to start anew.

For Bill the situation didn't end. On one side, the idea of federal police officers breaking the law demoralized him. What made this country the best in the world was the moral conscience of its citizens. Regardless of political affiliation, race, or creed, most Americans worked tenaciously to help maintain the ethical fabric which has sustained this country generation after generation. The other part was Mexican citizens arriving and arresting

American citizens. It was unacceptable: under no circumstances are foreign agents allowed to circumvent the American legal system and abduct United States citizens. As a former police officer Bill couldn't just let it go; he had to do something about it. But not right now.

Bill moved away from Julia and Frank, and walked toward the center of the room. He stood there for a few seconds, then went to the kitchen and grabbed kitchen and paper towels and walked back to the center of the room. After a quick glance around the room he announced, "I want you to inspect the walls and the floor of this room, inch by inch, and using paper towels, collect any items that belong to you. Then we need to wipe the chairs and any other surfaces that we touched. Let's do this quick—but let's be thorough. We need to clean everything we touched."

Hours later they were outside the trailer getting ready to leave. All the objects they collected from the floor was made into a bundle, along with the kitchen and paper towels, and then placed inside Bill's car trunk. Bill hugged Julia and Frank goodbye.

Before getting into his car Bill said to Frank, "Go home and get some rest, but I need you to get up early tomorrow morning and go to the Fallbrook house and clean it from top to bottom. Nobody should notice we were there."

Frank didn't answer, he just nodded.

Julia was still concerned about her safety and her liberty. "Bill, are you going to call the police?"

Bill did not answer right away; he was trying to frame his answer in a way that would make sense to all of them.

"No. I wouldn't be able to tell them what happened. There are too many pieces to this story. I honestly don't believe anybody else will be coming after us—today or tomorrow. Please go home and rest. Both of you have earned that much."

Without another word Bill got inside the car, turned on the engine, placed the car in reverse, and then drove it forward, down the narrow dirt road.

A minute later Frank's truck was also driving along the same dirt road.

Thirty-four

Rosarito, Baja California
Thursday December 24, 2009

For the last four days Angelica had tended to her everyday chores like any other wife and mother in Rosarito. After a difficult Monday morning she managed to regain her composure and find her strength to move on with her daily life. After her husband left for San Diego on Monday morning, she stayed in bed clutching a pillow close to her face to muffle her sobs. She cried until her ribs and abdomen ached from the convulsions, staining the pillow with tears and mucus. Drained of energy, she had fallen asleep, only to wake up and feel the tears flowing again. Without her husband she felt empty, catatonic, unable to focus on what to do. Tired, sad, and at times furious at her husband for placing her in this predicament, she had managed to shower, dry herself and change into a T-shirt and sweat pants. She fixed herself a cup of coffee, unplugged the phone and sat on the couch, looking out into the street from the living room window. As the morning unfolded and with tears running down her face again, she understood what Luis and Ramiro's wives felt when their husbands did not come home to them. There are so many unfinished words, regrets, acts of kindness and other things a wife wants to say to the departed husband, but she can't, because it's too late, because he has gone to a place where she can't follow. There were so many things she wished she had said, but how do you compile life's memories and feelings in a few sentences? She wondered what day of the week her husband would die, and if it would be a painful death. If Javier died would somebody inform her? Maybe Javier would die and his body would be dumped someplace, never to be found.

On Monday when her parents arrived they insisted on staying with her for the entire week; they wanted to provide moral support, help Angelica stay busy, and to be available in case she needed to leave the house at a moment's notice. Angelica refused. She needed to be alone.

On Tuesday morning after a light breakfast, Angelica called Teresa and asked her to go with her to visit Leticia, Ramiro's widow. Driving along

Avenida Juarez, Angelica and Teresa talked about being grateful to the faithful tourists for coming to visit Rosarito on a regular basis, to spend their money in spite of the increasing shootings between rival *narco-traficantes* groups. During their conversation Angelica tried to smile a couple of times but Teresa knew better; Angelica's drained face said it all. She was worried sick about her husband's whereabouts.

On Wednesday the three women went to the beach for a long walk, and later to the *Comercial Mexicana,* the town's version of a Wal-Mart, to buy books and art supplies for them and their families. They decided the best way to fight monotony was to stay busy and productive. Angelica bought drawing pencils and paper with the eagerness to start drawing again, as she did in her childhood years. She wanted to make a sketch of large branches of a tree with the ocean in the background. The rest of the day was uneventful, and the group made a list of the food and decorations they wanted to make to celebrate the arrival of Christmas and the New Year. She had intended to call David's mother but each time she picked up the phone she couldn't find the courage to dial the phone number. What could they possibly talk about? She was being selfish and she knew it, because deep down David's mother was also suffering from the same ailment. But Angelica was too drained of energy to talk about David and Javier.

At Leticia's house, they made fresh coffee. Sitting in the living room, holding a cup of coffee each, the women started talking about unemployment and the high cost of living, and its effects on the people of Rosarito, particularly those on a fixed income, like Teresa and Leticia. Angelica sat by herself in the middle of the sofa, Teresa and Leticia sat on reclining chairs facing Angelica. When the cups of coffee were consumed, the room became quiet. Teresa and Leticia knew the motive for Angelica's visit; both understood the pain and the feeling of nausea that comes when you lose somebody you love and you don't know what to do. For the two widows the pain and the nausea were still there, but they had managed to adapt, and at times control their emotions, especially in front of their children.

As if on cue, Angelica's head tilted forward and her shoulders started to sag. Unable to control her emotions, the tears started to flow. The empty cup of coffee dropped to the floor when Angelica raised her hands to cover her face. The sobbing became uncontrollable, her shoulders moving up and down, as if they were moving to the rhythm of a song. With her hands covering her face and her feet on the ground Angelica leaned on her right side, resting her head on a large pillow. Teresa came and sat next to her, gently rubbing her left shoulder. Leticia went to the kitchen to get a clean kitchen towel. Wetting the towel with warm water Leticia walked back to the couch, sat on her knees in front of Angelica, and waited for the moment to pass. When Angelica was ready she used the wet kitchen towel to clean her face.

They remained quiet, there was nothing to say.

Angelica was lost and she had come to find refuge with the people who had gotten lost, but had found their way again.

On Thursday morning Angelica got out of bed, took a quick shower and fixed herself a cup of coffee. It was almost seven o'clock in the morning. The house was quiet; the only sounds came from the family dog's feet moving about on the concrete steps in front of the house.

With a cup of coffee in her hand Angelica walked to the living room window and opened the curtains. Cars and people were beginning to move along the street. She sat on the couch looking out the window, lost in thought, drinking her coffee.

From the left side of the window Angelica saw a blue and white taxi make a left turn at the corner of the street. After making the turn, the taxi didn't accelerate, as they normally did. Instead, the taxi stopped in front of the house. From her window she saw the passenger in the backseat give the driver the cab fare. In a split second Angelica recognized Javier inside the taxi. She got up from the couch and headed towards the door, the cup of coffee dropping to the floor, spilling the contents on the carpet. Cautiously Angelica opened the door and stood outside; she was afraid she had made a mistake and had confused the passenger for her husband. When Javier got out of the taxi, Angelica covered her mouth with both of her hands, tears running down her face, unable to move. With a tired face and red eyes Javier walked to his wife and hugged her. Angelica didn't react to the hug. Still covering her mouth with her hands, the faces of Teresa and Leticia came to her mind. A primeval scream came from deep inside her soul; she had been given a second chance, a chance not afforded to her two sisters.

With a soothing voice Javier said, "It's over .. . we are done. David is safe at his home."

With her head buried in her husband's chest, Angelica didn't answer, she just nodded her head.

Thirty-five

Four days after Bill had crossed paths with the two Mexican police officers in a trailer tucked inside an avocado orchard on a cool December night, Bill's car crossed the Tijuana International Border checkpoint without a problem. After crossing the border checkpoint Bill saw the Rosarito exit sign. He made a right turn and followed the road along *Avenida International*, the long stretch of road where the Mexico-United States border fence is located. As he drove along the two-lane avenue he had the opportunity to see the Mexican side of the fence. On the left side of the avenue, old houses, abandoned vehicles, grime-covered buildings with broken windows, and businesses with faded signs adorned the dirty streets. In the distance cars drove by and people went about their business. On the right side young kids with ill-fitting clothes jumped and waved as cars drove by; single persons and groups congregated along the fence, particularly at places where sections of the fence had been removed or open holes were exposed. Sections of the metal fence, old and corroded by the passing of time, were adorned with graffiti.

The avenue started a steep climb and when Bill's vehicle reached the highest point along the avenue, where *Avenida International* changes into *Avenida Liberamento Sur*, over the fence, two U.S. Border Patrol vehicles came into view. Four officers, leaning against the hoods of their vehicles for support, used high-tech binoculars to keep track of the people congregating along the fence. Once Bill's car passed the highest point, the road dropped down and then made a sharp right turn onto *Autopista Playas de Tijuana*. Bill continued driving for another three miles and then the road turned into the *Autopista Escenica Tijuana-Ensenada* toll road. As the highway started to turn to the left, making a wide arc, the circular building, *El Toreo de Playas de Tijuana*, the Bullring-by-the-Sea, made an appearance. Bill slowed down when he approached the toll both. He paid the 1.90 U.S. dollars toll fee, then continued driving and twenty minutes later passed the *Punta Bandera Beach* and later the *Costa del Sol* exit signs. Five minutes later Bill saw the

Rosarito exit sign. Slowing down Bill left the highway toll road and drove along Avenida Juarez.

The street was saturated with liquor stores, restaurants, motels, curio shops, grocery stores, and street vendors. There was almost a stop sign or a traffic light at every corner, with speed bumps at short intervals. Cars of various sizes and models drove along the street, dodging pedestrians and traffic officers.

The town's local *fútbol* field was easy to spot: at different times, white *fútbol* balls rose above the long eight-foot high concrete wall, almost half a city block in length. Bill's car slowed down, made a right turn on *Calle Francisco Villa*, continued driving and stopped at the end of the street, on *Calle Rodolfo Sanchez*. Bill found a parking space, locked the car and walked to the entrance of the *fútbol* field. The entrance was being guarded by a teenage girl. He gave the girl a dollar to pay for the fifty-cent entrance fee, and continued walking; he didn't wait for the change.

Javier was easy to spot; he was standing along the four-foot high chain link fence, yelling at one of the soccer players on the field. There were plenty of people in the stands, mostly families. The teams were warming up, getting ready for a game.

Naturally, Javier turned towards the entrance and smiled as he saw Bill approaching. Javier walked towards Bill, and extended his hand. Bill reached out and shook hands with him.

Javier smiled and said, "Mr. Morgan—I knew you would come. I was hoping you would find the time to stop by and say hello. David is also here; let me get him." Javier turned and waved at David on the other side of the field. David waved back. Javier motioned for him to join them.

As David walked to join them, Javier went to the concession stand and bought three cold cans of Pepsi. Walking back he noticed David and Bill greeting each other. Javier gave each a soft drink, and standing along the fence, pretending to watch the players, they started to talk.

"Five years ago Luis Hernandez and Ramiro Flores were tortured and shot to death at Punta Bandera Beach, a few miles north of here," Javier paused to point north using the can of Pepsi. "Both were police officers, but more importantly, they were husbands and fathers." He paused again to take a drink from the can. Pointing to one of the players he said, "See that boy, the one passing the ball right now? That's Luis's grandson. See the goalkeeper? That's Ramiro's grandson. This is a small town, Bill; most of us are related." Javier paused to let Bill absorb the information.

"I became an orphan in my early teens, and I was sent to live here in Rosarito with my uncle and my aunt. I had lost my soul after my parents died. Luis was my cousin and with his help I found myself again. He saved my life. One weekend Luis and Ramiro went camping and didn't return. Tom, Sam, a banker and a group of Mexicans made a drug transaction at the same beach where Luis and Ramiro were camping. They were both tortured and then killed. Somebody in the group had the absurd idea to make it look like a drug transaction gone bad between two local police officers. For years the Hernandez and Flores families went through hell, physically and emotionally. They still do. The drug transaction stigma ruined both families financially; the families were denied the opportunity to collect insurance money or pension benefits. All of us paid a heavy price, Mr. Morgan."

Javier's eyes started to glisten.

The noise from screams and yells of the fans watching the game gave them a chance to rest. As they followed the game Bill had a chance to absorb the atmosphere of the place. He couldn't help but be moved by the families, couples, single people, teenagers, and children, laughing, cheering the players on.

Bill waited a few minutes for a pause in the game and then asked, "How did you find the federal agents?"

Smiling, Javier answered, "It was mostly luck, with lots of perseverance, and a few friends."

"I need to go back home but before I do, I need a favor," Bill kept quiet for a few seconds before continuing.

David and Javier looked at each other and then nodded in approval.

"Regardless of the heinous crimes the federal agents committed, their families are innocent bystanders, just like yours, and they need to have closure. Please tell me where the bodies of the agents are located so that I can inform the families."

David and Javier traded looks again. Javier approached Bill and said, "That's a fair request, Mr. Morgan. At this point there is no need to involve you or anybody else. I will make an anonymous call from here next week. If they trace the call, they are welcome to come and visit us."

"Thank you," Bill said.

"We also have a favor, Mr. Morgan," David asked.

"Go ahead," Bill answered, unsure of the request.

"It's about the banker. We don't want the banker to get away."

"I'll do what I can," Bill managed to say. He was caught off guard by the request.

David extended his hand to Bill. "Thank you for visiting, Mr. Morgan"

Bill shook hands with David and then with Javier.

"Once they find the bodies there will be uproar. Do you understand? The police, federal agencies, politicians, family members and the tabloids are going to have a field day. It's going to be a mess. Before this ends, I have a strong feeling they will be coming after both of you. Do you understand?"

Javier responded, "Maybe . . . Maybe not. Either way, we will wait here because we have no place to go. This is our home."

Bill left the *fútbol* field, got into his car and drove back home.

Thirty-six

The local NBC television affiliate station broke the news first, and then CNN carried the news nationwide. The local television station had received an anonymous phone call. The caller told the station where the bodies of the two missing federal agents were located. The station informed the police and they made a deal: the police were to handle the investigation, and when they were ready, the television station had the first rights to televise the details of the investigation.

The two bodies of the missing federal officers were found seven miles south of the town of Tecate. It was an empty, barren area. The autopsy report indicated the DEA agent had been shot twice, both times in the liver. The Border Patrol agent had been severely beaten before being shot twice, once in the liver and once in the chest. Both had their hands tied behind their backs and had been buried face up in shallow graves.

The two federal agents were hailed as heroes by the Border Patrol and DEA agencies. Two more brave agents had died in the line of duty. The San Diego City Mayor and local politicians called for a bigger police force; California congressmen and senators called for more Border Patrol agents, better equipment and a new high tech fence; the U.S. Attorney General made a promise to bring to justice the criminal, or criminals, that had committed the detestable crimes.

The funeral was a gut-wrenching event. It was painful to see family members hold each other, crying, hoping for honest answers that nobody was going to provide.

One week later, the deaths of the two federal agents started to fade. Wall Street problems, higher unemployment, federal and state budget problems, tornados, floods, daily suicide bombings in Iraq, the Taliban forces gaining strength in the Afghanistan-Pakistan border, high gas prices and the ongoing collapse of the housing market became top news.

After displaying a different attitude about himself, his work ethic, and a one-hour meeting with John, Frank received a promotion. John made Frank construction supervisor for the San Diego North County area. His responsibility was to make sure all the projects were completed on time and with superior workmanship.

After the promotion Frank proposed to Julia and she gladly accepted.

As Frank stated before, it was karma.

Finale

Throughout his life Bill had faced many personal dilemmas. Most of the time he managed to find the answer to the problem by simply having a courageous conversation with the other party over a cup of coffee. A few times, he went for long walks to clear his head; he would sit on a park bench and watch the people, the landscape, the sky, the sunset, and he would ask himself, what would my father have done in my place? The walks rejuvenated him; they gave him the energy to face the dilemma head on.

Bill got out of bed early, showered and then changed. He went to the kitchen and made a strong cup of Colombian coffee. Holding the cup of coffee he walked to the living room, sat on the couch, and leaning against cushions, he enjoyed every single drop of his coffee. From the coat closet he grabbed his jacket and from the small table by the front door he picked up the car keys. Without hurrying Bill got into his vehicle and driving at the posted speed limit, he drove for twenty minutes to the Saint Francis Church in Vista.

At this time of the morning the church was almost empty. He quietly walked inside the church and sat on one of the benches, near the altar. He sat and looked at the Christ on the cross. When he was ready he kneeled, bowed his head and prayed. In his prayers he revisited the situations with the federal agents as best he could. He prayed with the same devotion his mother and grandmother had taught him. With a serene feeling in his soul he got up, slowly walked out of the church, and then drove back home in silence; his conscience was clear and his fortitude was strong.

At home he placed the car keys back on the table and the jacket inside the coat closet. He went to his desk and from one of the drawers he pulled out an address book and flipped through the pages until he found the phone number he was looking for. He picked up the phone and dialed the number. After three rings somebody answered, "Good morning, North County Times. How may I help you?"

"John Windlow, please."

"I will connect you. One moment, please."

"Hello, this is John Windlow."

"Hi, John, this is Bill Morgan."

"Bill, how are you!"

"I am fine, John."

"How can I be of service, Bill?"

"John, I have a story that would be of interest to you."

"OK. Care to elaborate a bit more?"

"All I can say is this, you will not be disappointed."

"Fair enough, Bill. When do you want to talk?"

"This morning, if you can."

"OK. Give me an hour."

"I'll have the coffee ready. And John, please bring lots of pencils and paper, you will need them."

"See you in an hour, Bill."

After placing the phone receiver down Bill walked down the hallway towards the garage. In the garage he found three, white letter-size storage cardboard boxes. One by one, the boxes were collected, carried to the kitchen and placed on the table. The lids of the boxes were removed to expose the contents. One box contained the plastic bag with the bloody flashlight, the computer floppy disks, Sam's set of keys and Julia's bloody clothes. Another box contained the material Bill, Frank and Julia had collected after cleaning Chino's trailer days ago. The last box contained the notes and recording material from Julia's interview.

Bill walked to the kitchen counter and made a fresh pot of coffee. When the coffee started brewing he walked to the living room and sat on the couch facing the television set. Using the remote control he turned the television on and then flipped through the channels until he found the local news. Bill placed the remote control next to him and then waited for the coffee to finish brewing, and for the arrival of John Windlow.